MAKING WAVES

LORDS OF THE ABYSS

MICHELLE M. PILLOW

MICHELLE M. PILLOW® - MICHELLEPILLOW.COM

When Demon, a merman tasked with patrolling the ocean for humans in distress, comes across a woman anchored to the bottom of the sea, he's sure his dreams have come true. After all, she's stunning, single, and makes his body burn with need. She's also impetuous, being hunted by his enemies, and seriously conflicted on whether or not he's a good guy. It's his duty to not only protect her, but to win her heart—because this lonely merman is sure she's the one for him. Now he just has to convince her.

The Mighty Hunter
Commanding the Tides
Captive of the Deep
Surrender to the Sea
Making Waves
The Merman King

The Playful Prince
The Bound Prince
The Rogue Prince
The Pirate Prince

Captured by a Dragon-Shifter Series

Determined Prince
Rebellious Prince
Stranded with the Cajun
Hunted by the Dragon
Mischievous Prince
Headstrong Prince

Space Lords Series

His Frost Maiden
His Fire Maiden
His Metal Maiden
His Earth Maiden
His Woodland Maiden

Dynasty Lords Series

Seduction of the Phoenix
Temptation of the Butterfly

To learn more about the Qurilixen World series of
books and to stay up to date on the latest book list
visit www.MichellePillow.com

DEDICATION

To My Readers

1

THIS WAS HELL.

Victoria had no doubts about that simple fact. The rental boat she'd taken out on vacation had sunk, she'd drowned, and for her sins she'd been sent to hell. It wasn't fire and brimstone. It was the endless abyss, the dark depths of the ocean—cold and lonely and wet.

She was trapped at the bottom of the world, impossibly aware of her surroundings, unable to breathe anything but the salty brine. It turned out heaven wasn't as lenient as some would have her believe, because a greater power had condemned her into the watery prison for playing a little too loose with her tax deductions, and calling Becky Gibson a bitch in the third grade, and any number of things she had considered small infractions at the time.

Sorry Becky.

And she found she *was* sorry. Victoria had a lot of time to think about it. She was sorry for a great many things these days. Or weeks? She couldn't be sure. Time was not kept in the deep ocean, not like onshore.

Something flitted by her vision and she stiffened. Victoria waited, the sickening feeling curling through her stomach to tell her that this was it—some grand finale to end her horrible journey through death. The monsters were going to come nibble on her again— horrible little fish with sharp teeth and glowing dots hanging from their heads. All she could do was thrash about until they went away or she became too tired to fight.

She'd seen a couple of larger creatures, but thankfully they stayed in the distance, passing like shadows within a shadow. Tentacles skimmed sand, stirring clouds that looked like nightmares. She had to concentrate in the darkness to see them, her eyesight focused like the beams of two flashlights with a limited field of vision.

Other creatures crawled beneath her through the pasture of flowing seagrass...or was it moss, or a fungus that crawled up from dark places? Once, a line of translucent lobsters with giant claws had marched past. She felt more than saw them, but tried not to move, not wanting them to notice her floating in the abyss like a meal on a string. Long, thin worms drifted with the currents and she tried to avoid touching them.

The fear of things she couldn't see was worse than the dangers lurking in the waters.

Demons.

They called themselves Olympians and acted like goddesses, but Victoria found nothing godly about their glowing eyes and unnatural coloring, or the way they'd pulled her into the water to drown her a second time—as if the first death had not been enough torture. They'd said many things when they'd held her prisoner at Mt. Olympus, but she'd been so dazed, coming in and out of focus as they spoke, that very little had registered.

Yep. This is hell, and the Ancient Greeks run it.

And the ugly fish with their razor teeth.

And the darkness. Endless darkness.

Victoria had become a strange and slimy plant. She was tethered by her waist, fastened to the seabed with a thick chain that was her stem. And her leaves were the silky fins where her feet used to be. She missed her feet. She missed her legs. Now there was a fish tail—useless because she couldn't even kick with it.

In the distance, she detected a large dome, sunken into the water like a snow globe some kid had dropped and forgotten. The Olympian demons who had planted her said that she should try to make it back to the dome, like a test rigged for her to fail. Yet, it was her only chance at salvation.

Well, *said* was too incorrect of a word. They didn't use their mouths to speak. Instead they implanted the thoughts of what they were saying in her head.

The best Victoria could reason is that if she made it to the dome, she'd become a demon like the women who'd brought her here. They all had tails, too. Had they been like her once? A lost soul trying to reason with the unknown?

Her thoughts drifted like ocean currents, making it harder for her to quantify events so she could fathom what had happened. Conclusions came to her, but it was as if they'd already been formed and forgotten like waves that had been washed ashore, useless, and pointless upon reflection.

Mermaids? Demons?

Was she a mermaid? She looked at her tail, and

then at the ugly fins that jutted from her once smooth arms.

The light from the dome caught her attention yet again and her thoughts drifted to salvation. Familiar darkness or the light of the unknown?

Anything was better than the constant fear residing in her chest, and the oppressive icy silence of ocean water.

Deep ocean. Mortals don't come here. Therefore, I am not mortal, she thought.

Victoria flung her arms back and forth, trying to pull herself through the water. Each inch was hard fought. After she managed to move several feet, she couldn't pump her arms anymore. Water entered and expelled from her lungs, the feeling heavy and uncomfortable. She fought to move again, resting and fighting, fighting and resting. Two feet. Four feet. One foot. An inch.

Victoria opened her mouth to scream, but the water kept her in silence.

No more.

Please, no more.

I'm sorry, Becky.

I didn't mean to cheat on my test, Mrs. Larsen. I swear I saw the answer by accident.

I'll clean my room.

I'm sorry I threw away perfectly good food. I know other kids are starving and would be grateful for your tuna noodle casserole, Mom.

I miss my parents. I'll call them more often.

I'll not take deductions on my taxes.

I'll not swear, or watch bad movies, or drink, or tell indecent jokes.

I'll volunteer more.

So many sins...

No more, please.

I don't know what else there could be.

No more.

2

DEMON GRABBED Cain by his arm, throwing the Merr hunter so that he was propelled ahead. Together, they glided above the ocean floor. In his sights was the Olympian mermaid Pirene, who they had discovered swimming in open water. Damn mermaids were a nuisance. Both men would much rather be hunting the water spirits that attacked boats from the surface world. At least the scylla didn't know what they were doing and, though very dangerous, they were predictable in their mindlessness.

The strength of Demon's toss forced Cain past the treacherous mermaid like a yellow javelin, allowing the man time to turn around and face her. As Cain stopped her retreat, Demon came up from behind to trap Pirene between them.

Dark blue fins and brown hair fluttered in the water as Pirene tried to change directions. The mermaid was a loyal Olympian, following the teachings of her egocentric, pain-in-the-fin queen, Maia. Pirene made a hissing noise of irritation over the mind link as Cain darted for her.

'*Stop, by order of King Lucius,*' Demon commanded. All Merr communicated by telepathy in the water and he knew the woman heard him clearly. He was annoyed, being forced to patrol the waters outside the dome. As a hunter, and a member of the team nicknamed the *Warriors*, he was usually set free in the ocean waters to track scylla—not bored mermaids with demented ideas of overthrowing the king and taking control of their underwater world of Atlantes.

'*I recognize no king.*' Pirene swam erratically, darting left and right, up and down.

'*What are you doing out here, Pirene? You know it is forbidden.*' Cain kept his tone calm. '*Come back with us to the palace and let's see if we can't start a conversation to end this nonsense. Don't you think our world is fractured enough? We should be working together to end the curse, not apart.*'

Demon gave Cain credit for trying to speak reason, but even before Pirene answered, he knew it was useless. There was no negotiating with traitors, especially ones like the Olympians. The rumors surfacing over the last ten years about their actions were what his brother Rigel's new wife would call cringe-worthy.

All knew merfolk were very sexual creatures and received much of their power from sexual release, but the Olympians took it a step further. Instead of using the pleasure nymph dolls created to ease the loneliness of eternity for those without mates, they lured humans to the ocean, brought them below to Atlantes, and then treated them like slaves.

'*I answer to Queen Maia.*' Pirene made a direct line for the dome. '*You would do well to bow down to her now, hunters, and perhaps she will reward you with a place on her palace floor once she is on the Atlas throne.*'

Cain laughed, the mocking sound filling the mind link. '*What do you think, Demon, would you like to be a rug for Maia to walk on?*'

'*No thanks,*' Demon answered. '*I've heard how she treats people.*'

'*How dare you speak—*' Pirene didn't have a chance to finish. As if sensing the danger, the giant guard worm that lived within the rocky base of the Atlantes dome surged forward. The gelatinous creature didn't have much in the way of a face, only a rounded tip with an elastic mouth that could swallow prey whole. Echoes of a scream were instantly crushed as the worm sucked Pirene into his mouth and kept swimming.

The worm moved close to Demon. He lifted a hand to pet the ancient beast. The creature returned to his home as quickly as he left.

'Did you call him?' Cain asked.

'No,' Demon answered. He might not like Pirene, but he wouldn't have chosen to kill her. The mermaid should have known the danger at the dome's base.

'I guess we're not taking her prisoner,' Cain thought wryly.

There were only so many ways a Merr could end their immortality and that was one of them. Perhaps Pirene had psychically called the worm on herself.

'Please tell me our patrol is over. I want nothing more than to get back to the ocean, away from these irrational females.' Cain flicked his tail and shot toward the dome so that he could look inside at their contained world. His hand slid over the transparent, smooth surface as if to caress those below.

There was no penetrating the hard dome barrier, which was fortunate, or else the tiny paradise would be flooded. Although those within would shift into Merr form in ocean water, they would be cursed to wander. After a few weeks in the briny depths, they would become insane, transforming into ocean spirits known as the scylla—a fate worse than death. Inside the dome was the only air the Merr could breathe and doing so kept them from turning. This ensured they always returned home.

Above them, the dome disappeared into the black waters of the deep, forming what was Atlantes' sky. Tiny animals were drawn to the warmth, swimming to the barrier during the Merr night to form dancing sea stars over the borders.

The dome sat upon a rocky base that supported the land within. While inside, the Merr didn't feel the dome move, but it drifted with the currents, gliding across the ocean floor. Over the centuries, Demon had watched Atlantes' slow progression through various underwater landscapes.

An air bubble trapped within the sea, self-contained with mild seasons, land animals, and a people who clung to the culture they had known on Earth, one might say Atlantes was magical.

For all the magic and beauty, Atlantes was nothing more than a curse. Only a god could create such a prison, and that is exactly what had happened.

They had been human once—arrogant and stupid and vain. Poseidon punished them, turning them into the Merr and sinking them beneath the waves.

To swim to the surface and breathe the air above meant death—well, traditionally it did. Lady Bridget, a scientist they'd rescued from drowning, was working on a cure she believed was tied to deep-ocean seaweed. When Demon's twin brother, Brutus, had been pushed above the ocean's surface, his skin had survived the brief contact when he should have burst into flames.

That didn't mean any of them were willing to take a big gulp of human air anytime soon.

From some of the items they'd recovered from the surface world, Demon knew that their broken piece of land would no longer fit. If they were suddenly to rise from the ocean and walk again on land, they would no longer be the great kings and warriors they once were. Their empire had fallen and their gods had disappeared into myths. To humans, Merr would be no more than curiosities and pets. The few humans they'd managed to save and bring down reported that the Greek gods were dead, no longer feared or worshiped.

Which meant the curse could never be lifted. Poseidon had stopped watching them.

What choice was there but to continue on?

Demon had no desire to die. He hunted because it was a prestigious position in his society, and a way to get out of the dome. Men like Cain hunted in hopes the gods would somehow see the many human lives they tried to save from drowning when the scylla attacked ships.

There were twelve hunters in total, split up into four teams of three. Demon's team, the *Warriors*, included his twin Brutus and their younger brother Rigel. Cain led the *Knights*. Hrafn led the *Soldiers*, who had not been in the water for a long time. The fourth team was simply called the *Hunters*, two members of which had rescued human women and married them.

That was another reason Demon hunted—in hopes of rescuing a woman who would choose him as a husband. The odds were not great, but Brutus and Rigel had somehow managed it. Seeing his brothers happy made Demon feel lonelier, and he hated himself for secretly resenting their joy.

'*One inch.*'

Demon frowned. '*What?*'

'*I have no more inches in me. Get it over with, demon fish.*'

Demon looked around the open water to find who was speaking. 'Who's talking to me? Cain?'

'That wasn't me,' Cain answered. 'It's a female. By all the gods, is there another one of them out here? I swear, we plug one of their escape routes and they find another.'

'Demon, demon of the sea, come back for me.' The words were filled with a plea and followed by a half-crazed laugh.

'Who's calling me?' Demon demanded, irritated by this new game the Olympians were playing.

'Perhaps they're within the dome?' Cain offered, peering down at the countryside below.

Demon started to swim toward the transparent barrier to look down upon the dry world within, but her voice only became sadder and disorientated.

'I can't do it. I don't know how to swim. I'm done, demon fish, I'm done. You can have me, Becky.'

Granted, the Olympians were completely insane, but their insanity all had the same tyrannical ring to it—they were superior, they were not going to live under the domination of a man, they were goddesses of whatever. They never sounded defeated.

Something caused him to turn and consider the open ocean. He scanned above before slowly searching below. Movement drifted in the distant water.

'Found her,' Demon said in irritation. Even though he was annoyed, the thrill of the chase filled him and gave him a burst of energy. He darted forward to catch the Olympian before she could get away. Though he expected her to try, the mermaid didn't attempt to evade capture.

'Demon, do you need help?' Cain asked.

'No.' Demon slowed. Detecting the glint of metal holding the woman down, he quickly glanced around to see if it was a trap. A long line cut through the ocean floor, ending at an old ship anchor holding the chained mermaid down. Was this Olympian punishment? Had this mermaid betrayed her queen?

Brunette hair floated around her head, shorter than most Olympians wore their locks. The green fins indicated her eyes would most likely be the same shade. If nothing else, Demon was sure he would have recognized the curves of her body. A man didn't forget curves like that.

He approached her cautiously. The black of his fins and tail made him particularly hard to detect in the deep ocean. He lifted his arm, creating a small current of water to force her hair from her face.

Glassy eyes met his. The almost translucent green didn't appear to register him swimming before her.

He'd seen that look before in the scylla they had brought back from the hunt, right before the poor creatures died.

Demon glanced down at the chain, realization hitting him. She'd been left to turn. She would have been alone in the water for a very long time to be in this state.

'*Cain,*' Demon cried.

'*I thought you said you had her,*' Cain teased, even as he came to help.

'*Quick, she's turning into a scylla,*' Demon said.

All humor left Cain as he dashed forward. '*But we're right by the dome. How could she have been lost at sea?*' Cain's question was answered for him when he saw Demon jerking at the chain.

'*I can't free her. Help me pull her.*' Demon hooked his arm under the woman's shoulders and held her tight as he swam as hard as he could toward home. Cain held the chain, trying to take the weight off the mermaid's waist.

'*I don't want to be a demon,*' the mermaid mumbled through the mind link, though her eyes were still vacant. '*I don't want to hurt anyone, lounging on a pillow, watching them die.*'

'*Do you know her? I don't recognize her,*' Cain said. '*She keeps saying your name but nothing else makes sense to me.*'

'No.' Demon had no idea how the woman knew who he was.

'*Demon, I don't think she's going to make it,*' Cain said. '*Look at her skin. She's too far gone.*'

Demon didn't answer as he swam harder. An old fear and sadness knotted his insides. Too many had died this way, too many that he'd carried back from the abyss.

3

DEMON BROKE the surface of the water, still holding the chained woman. Even shifted, he was able to take deep breaths of dome air. The sweet smell of Crystal Caves was always the first thing to greet him when he came home. He would know that smell anywhere.

The caves were accessible from the palace of Atlas, the capital of Ataran, in the Atlantean dome, far below the world of the humans above. Pressure kept the ocean water from flooding in through the base. This was supposed to be the only surfacing area into the dome, but the pesky Olympians kept burrowing through. Seeing the woman's translucent skin threaded with blue lines, Demon wanted to hunt the mermaid monsters and strangle each and every one of them. There were some boundaries that didn't get crossed and turning merfolk into scylla was one of them.

"We should take her to Althea. The healer will know what to do with her," Cain said, able to use his voice now that he was out of the water. He brushed the liquid from his tail so that it broke apart and shifted back into two legs. The gills on his neck molded into skin, and the sharp fins along his forearms retracted. "Try to pull her from the water. I'll find something to cut her free."

Cain pushed up from the ground, not bothering to find clothes as he ran toward the palace entrance where the guard would be stationed. None of the hunters worried about nudity since they never wore clothes in the ocean.

Demon held the woman with one arm as he braced his free hand to push his body out of the ocean. With a flip of his tail, he hopped onto the rocky ledge, lifting her so that she sat next to him in the shallow water lapping the rim of the cave floor. She hung limp, draped over his arm. The sharp edge of her fin cut his upper tail as her arm slipped to the side. Blood ran from the injury into the water, but he ignored the sharp sting of saltwater on the wound.

Demon pushed up a tier onto dry land, again sliding her along with him. The tingling of a shift was slow to come as he tried to brush the droplets of water off his scales. It wasn't easy while holding the chained mermaid. The bottom of her tail still dipped into the dark water. After some maneuvering, he managed to dry the saltwater enough that scales could shift into flesh.

When he could again stand as a man, he found it easier to lift her onto land. He laid her on her back. A dark bruise had formed around her waist where the chains held her tight. He followed the links, pulling at their unbreakable metal until he found a small lever. In the dark water, it would have been impossible to see. Pushing it, he was able to unhook the weight from her body. The anchor pulled the chains fast, and he grabbed her as the heavy metal whipped from her waist, snapping the side of the cave before being dragged into the water. The raw skin where the chain scraped against her should have bled, but it merely maintained a pale pink color amongst the blue-tinted flesh.

Demon lifted her into his arms. His wet black hair clung to his shoulders. The sound of water dripping on the floor punctuated his every step as he rushed her to see the healer. Gemstones covered the walls surrounding them, giving the surfacing area the name Crystal Caves. The colorful stones reflected the torchlight coming from the entrance, helping him to see as he climbed up the slope away from the water.

Her naked body felt cold in his arms, not unusual for a Merr coming out of the ocean. Her legs did not readily shift from the tail, but her sharp fins retracted by small degrees into her forearms. The feel of a woman's naked body had become foreign to him. Centuries had passed since he'd been with anything but a pleasure nymph, built as a repository more than companionship. He still dreamed of it, but the idea had become a distant concept rather than an actual memory.

Her tail began to change color, still not the natural flesh of a woman, but at least she was shifting into her land legs. The slide of her wet skin caused a surge of desire to rack his body. The sexual affliction was always the worst when the Merr first came out of the ocean. Holding the woman became torturous, and he had yet to make it to the cave entrance.

"My lord, were you able to get her free or is this another one?" Brennus, the guard, asked as Demon approached. "Cain and Gaius have gone to Aidan to find something to cut chains."

The man was training to be a hunter though there were currently no openings on any of the teams. But, with the number of men who had recently found mates in the water, that might change, and King Lucius had decided it was time to start training those who might take their places.

Demon couldn't imagine ever giving up hunting. Getting out of the dome was what had kept him sane during their exile from the surface world.

Brennus' uniform consisted of the traditional Ionic *chiton*, which was a white rectangular piece of material folded in half, sewn up the sides, and pinned at the sleeves to create a knee-length shirt. The legs were left bare and, like most of the Merr, he wore the same style of strapped sandals they'd been wearing since they were first banished into the ocean. His green *chlamys* cloak draped over one shoulder where it was pinned with a circular gold brooch engraved with the ancient Merr symbol of the sun.

"Hand me your cloak," Demon ordered, eyeing the green material. The mermaid's scales were still showing in patches on her damp skin.

Brennus instantly obeyed, unhooking the brooch and sweeping the material off his body. "Is there another in the cave? Should I retrieve—?"

"It is only she," Demon answered as he adjusted the woman in his arms. Brennus laid the material over her. He hoped heat might help her finish the transformation back. "I was able to pull her free. When Cain returns, inform him I have taken her to the healer."

Brennus gave the woman a strange look. "Cain said that she was an Olympian? Do you know her?"

"No." Demon bounced her in his arms.

"So then it is true. The Olympians are drowning humans and bringing them down here to build their numbers." Brennus rolled a large round stone in front of the cave opening to block it off and keep any intruders from finding their way inside.

Demon didn't answer as he hurried down the hall.

"My lord," Brennus called after him. "What's wrong with her? She doesn't look right. She almost looks as if she is turning into a..."

Brennus' words trailed off. Demon frowned, walking faster as he finished the guard's observation for himself. "A scylla."

An immortal lifetime of teachings told him that her fate was out of his hands. If she lived it would be because the gods wanted her to. But, what if there were no gods? Or if there were, what if they simply didn't care either way?

Demon walked faster. He had to save her. Gods or no gods, law or no law, he had to try. This mermaid was no different from any human woman they had saved from the top. Since women were rare, honor required that he attempt to save their lives if he found one condemned to a watery death. Normally, that meant humans who already faced a death sentence by drowning in the ocean. They had often tried to save humans, only to have them perish on the dive into the abyss. This woman was already in the water, already transformed, so that had to mean she had a fighting chance. Right?

Althea the Healer would know what to do to save her. She was their only hope.

4

VICTORIA FELT SAFE, and warmer than she had in days, or weeks, or perhaps months. There was no way to mark the passing of time in hell. Arms held her, giving comfort where there had only been coldness before. Oh, and to be dry after so long in the wet. She had never thought she'd love being wrapped in a thick blanket so much.

Which of course meant she was with the devil. This was the false security, the tempting comfort, before they snatched it away from her again. The demons had done it before, singing sweet songs to her like sirens before shoving her chained body into the water to drown.

Her eyes opened, expecting to see black stone and fire.

Instead, the walls were constructed of large glazed bricks tinted with the blue color of the Mediterranean Sea, accented with yellow and white tiles. They passed a torch affixed to the wall, and the sight of fire confirmed she had been right about the devil.

Victoria tried to look at the man carrying her, but she couldn't move her head. She wanted to fight, to stand up and run, but her limbs hung like dead weights. Her eyes followed the intricate tiles as they created Greek patterns on the walls. They passed through an arch.

Her escort bounced her in his arms, adjusting his hold. Her head turned, and she stared up at a hand-some face. Black hair clung to a strong jaw and even stronger chest. He glanced down at her and his black eyes glinted with a sheen of silver. She tried to speak, but her throat was as frozen as her body.

"I have you," the devil said, his voice just as rough as she'd imagined it to be.

The low tone of his voice caused a passionate surge to wash over her body. Surely, he meant some-thing sinister with that statement, but her body responded as if he meant to take her right there in the hall, back pressed against the glazed stones, tight body pumping, thick cock claiming, bodies fucking.

Victoria pictured the scenario so vividly her sex actually ached for it to happen. The frustrating need held her in its torturous grip. Perhaps this was the devil's torment—a sexual desire so hot and so unfulfilled, it made her want to cry out in agony. She tried to move again but couldn't. Her flesh tingled, hot little sparks of pleasurable torture.

"Lady Althea," the devil called out. A beaded curtain crashed over her body, running along her as he carried her through without parting the strands. The feel of them caressed her, only making the sensations worse. "I need you to attend a Merr."

"Lord Demon, what do—" A woman's voice came to an abrupt stop.

"She was in the water," Demon stated.

"I would imagine so," Althea answered. "But what do you expect me to do with it? Take the poor creature to the scylla cells and let her find peace there. Then come back so I can tend to that cut on your thigh. It looks deep."

"She's not a scylla," Demon protested. Victoria felt him carry her deeper into the room. "She's a mermaid. I found her in the water. She was chained. See, the red on her waist? She is still Merr."

The demon laid her on a low couch and she was thankful to stop moving. Ocean currents drifted endlessly and there was no stillness in the water. If she couldn't have the fantasy boiling inside her body, she wanted to lie in this comfortable spot forever. The heat of sexual desire cooled as the man's hands left her.

"Not on my furniture," Althea scolded.

From what Victoria could see, the healer was a slender woman. She wore a shiny gown of light teal with darker edges. Two pins held the dress together at the shoulders to create thin straps. Brown hair wound her head to form a crown of hair.

"Demon, please, she's all wet, and scylla never leave this world well. Take her to the holding cells. Gregor can help ease her suffering better than I."

"I'm not taking her to the cell," Demon stated. "Will you help her or not?"

'*Thank you,*' Victorian thought, glad for more time on the cushions.

"At least take this and get me a real blanket. This damp cloak is not drying anything. Wait, did you...?" Althea asked with a gasp. "Was that her?"

The sound of footsteps on a hard floor erupted around her. She felt hands on her face and neck. That's when she realized she was completely naked. Victoria was no prude, but she also wasn't accustomed to lounging around without clothing, especially when others could see her. Unfortunately, she couldn't move to cover herself.

"Can you hear me?" the healer asked.

'*Shirt*,' Victoria thought.

The hands didn't leave her face, but Victoria felt a blanket of some sort being pulled up her body to cover her chest. The demon must have covered her. That seemed a strange thing for a demon to do.

"She will live," Demon stated as if he held command over life and death. "And she is not a scylla. She is a mermaid."

"She's not from here," Althea answered, her hands still moving over Victoria's face in the strangest manner. It was almost as if the healer's fingers sent vibrations into her brain to read Victoria's thoughts. "You know that, don't you? She comes from above. She's new, too, not even half a year down, less than that for her transformation from human to Merr. What are those Olympians thinking? Why would they purposefully drag people down to our existence? Do they think to overpopulate the dome? And why would they then turn those people into scylla? Can Queen Maia be that coldhearted?"

"The transformation did something to Maia," Demon said. "I think the coldness of the abyss was too much for her. She broke inside."

"You would be the only one who thinks so," Althea mused. "I thought you hunters had those sea witches contained?"

"They keep finding new tunnels." Demon's words sounded defensive and a little irritated.

"You realize this makes her your ward." The healer's hands moved away from her face.

"No, it doesn't," Demon denied. "I don't know anything about taking care of a ward. I'll bring her to my brothers. They have wives. They will know how to care for a—"

"It doesn't work like that," Althea laughed, "and you know it. She's all yours, my lord. Congratulations. And lest I forget, Aidan has gone to the countryside, so you're going to have to acclimate her to Atlas yourself. He's not here to explain the way of things to her if she has an irrational reaction to this reality. Though, if I had my guess, I'd say she's already been given a big dose of our reality."

"But, I can't keep her with me. I'll break her," Demon still protested. "Can't you...?"

"The only thing I can do is help you with that cut. As for your affliction and your ward, those are both matters that you need to attend to yourself, Lord Demon. I can't help you with either."

"But—"

"I'm with Aidan so will not be easing anyone's affliction but his. Find a pleasure nymph. As to this woman, there is nothing more I can do."

'*Stillness.*' Victoria tried not to listen to their bickering. She was powerless to contribute to the conversation of her fate and sleep sounded wonderful. She wanted little more than to fall into nothingness—sweet, sweet, blessed nothingness.

5

Demon stood on the shower platform in his bathing room, pumping his hand over his hard affliction as the warm, fresh water rained down over him to wash away the salt and blood. He didn't even pause long enough to fetch soap. The Merr did not transform in fresh water, only the ocean. The healer's hands were nothing short of magic, and the cut on his thigh had begun to heal. But she was right, there was nothing else Althea could do for him—especially for his affliction.

He lived in the hunters' section of the palace in one of the twelve apartments set up for them. Each hunting team had a hall, and each man his own place. It kept them close together in times of work. He knew the apartments of his brothers were empty as they were at their country homes with their wives. That left him with few options as to what to do with his ward. The best thing might be to get permission from King Lucius to take her to the country and place her at the feet of one of his new sisters-by-marriage. They had been human much more recently than he.

His cock ached as it always did when he came back from a long swim. Only, for some reason, this time it felt more urgent. Holding the soft flesh of a woman had shaken him to the core, knocking loose a piece of fear he couldn't push away. What if he hurt her? She was so soft, so delicate, so...

Demon groaned, unable to help himself. His hands had slid against her wet body as he'd carried her. And, to his shame, he'd wanted to do things—wicked, naughty things. That is why she couldn't be his ward. He didn't trust himself to care for her properly. It had taken everything in him to ignore the images in his head urging him to press her up against the wall and sink his affliction in deep and hard and repeatedly like some angry beast.

He fisted both hands over his cock and rocked his hips. As much as it shamed him, he couldn't stop thinking about the woman—in his arms, exposed on the couch, breasts, thighs, thatch of hair guarding her sex, lips, mouth...*fuck!*

He pumped harder, so focused on his affliction that the feel of hands gliding along his back took him by surprise.

He slipped on the wet platform, and his hands slid off his erection. He stumbled, placing his hands on the wall to keep from falling. Before he could stand upright, the hands were once again on his flesh, moving along his back and ass. Demon held very still, unsure how to react.

The woman's wet, naked body glided along his as she came around the front. Her skin still held the translucent coloring, but her eyes were more aware. Her large breasts lifted as she panted for air, the hard nipples dancing along his skin as she came closer.

"The...affliction...my..." He tried to explain what he'd been doing, but the words were a jumbled mess as he was helpless against her actions.

Her fingers practically clawed his shoulders as she pushed him down. The slats of the platform cut into his ass. She pressed against the wound on his leg, but he didn't care as she lowered herself onto him. The lush curves of her body, the soft pressure of her skin, all of it captivated him.

Almost instantly, she slid herself onto his wet

arousal. The shower poured over them, gluing their hair to their bodies. Droplets rained into her mouth, only to trail out as she closed her lips. The seductive gesture was more than he could take.

Demon grabbed her hips, lifting her up and bringing her down hard. She didn't speak, didn't cry out, even as her lips parted wide and her hands dug into his chest. This was no synthetic pleasure nymph doll. When she kept moving, he let go of her hips and reached for her breasts. He wanted to flip her over and pin her beneath him, but she had him trapped between her wonderful thighs and he didn't dare move lest she stopped pumping up and down on him.

Her thrusts became almost angry as if she sought to punish him with each greedy push. Demon couldn't resist, couldn't hold back his release. He spilled his seed as she was still rocking over him. He tensed and every muscle stiffened. She rocked several more times before she too froze. The sound of the water hitting flesh punctuated the long moments before she finally moved off him.

What just happened?

He glanced down at his lowered arousal. It was as if she'd sucked the life right out of him. Green eyes met his through the falling water, rounded and confused. She gazed down at him. The tone of her flesh had filled in some, but had not completely turned back to a normal shade.

So many strange feelings welled inside of him, and he was slower to stand. The wound on his leg stung as he moved, having been aggravated by their lovemaking. "You are so..."

Her eyes widened even more, and she took a step back.

"Beautiful," he finished, not able to think of a more adequate word. There were so many thoughts swirling in his head that he couldn't grasp them to form a sentence, let alone a conversation. "Love."

Her eyes turned down to the floor as if trying to understand what she'd done.

"I'm sorry. I didn't realize you were suffering from the affliction as well. I should have known, but..."

Her eyes darted back up to his. She opened her mouth but still no sound came out. Demon pulled the shower cord and the rain stopped. He went to a basket on a shelf and pulled out drying linens. He offered her one, but she didn't readily move to accept it.

"Did they explain what this place is?" he asked.

She shook her head before taking the linen.

'*Can you hear me?*' he tried, using telepathy.

She continued to stare at him, not indicating that she did.

"This is my home," he said, motioning around the shower, before gesturing out of the bathing room into the main part of his apartment. "We are in the royal palace in Atlas. It's a city. We call our country Ataran. Have you heard of it?"

She again shook her head, not taking her eyes off him.

"You're in Atlantes. Have you heard of Atlantes?" Demon tried to gesture to help her understand. He drew his hands from overhead downward. "Underneath the ocean."

She looked up at his ceiling. At least she seemed to comprehend his words.

He arched his arms in the shape of the dome. "We are inside the water, in an air pocket. You're safe here."

She again turned her attention fully to him.

"I am Demon," he said.

At that, her eyes narrowed, and she began inching her way around him toward the door.

"I'm a *Warrior*," he tried to explain, turning in a circle to watch her. He wasn't sure where she was trying to go. His home was designed like the others in the palace. Off the bathing room, he had a large square living area with low couches. Next to that was an office he rarely used and a sleeping room. "I hunt with my brothers. We take women from the surface and bring them down to—"

His words cut off as she ran from him.

He darted after her. He heard a crash and made it to the door to see she had tripped on his couch and knocked over a vase. She crawled across the floor, the drying linen trailing after her as she tried to move and hold on to it at the same time.

"If you're worried about the sex, it is all right. We had the affliction. I always become particularly aroused after being in the ocean. I see it is the same for you. I am willing to let you use me like that again, should you still have a need." He smiled hopefully as he glanced down to where his arousal was pushing against the drying linen. Seeing her crawl had been particularly arousing, especially when the material fell away from her lush backside.

"Afflic..." The woman tried to speak. It was obvious that a combination of being physically weak and unsure of her surroundings had caused confusion. She backed up until she pressed against the door.

"It is what we call our unreleased sexual desires. Affliction." He stepped around the broken vase. It was a shame. He'd had the piece for over a thousand years. "If the Merr—that is who we are—don't find release, the tension builds inside of us and turns to anger and aggression. Fights break out and it is not pleasant for anyone."

She arched a brow.

"There is nothing like an affliction release to bring the levels inside us back to normal," he continued. "Perhaps if we try again, you will feel better and be able to speak?"

The side of her lip curled, but he didn't think it was in acceptance of his offer.

"Many are convinced this is yet another punishment from the gods. To be cursed with so many desires, but to have very few options in the way of lovers. Thousands of years tend to create a lot of drama between couples, and between lovers. It is easier to only be with a mate."

Her mouth opened and closed several times before she managed to say, "Dead."

"No, you're transformed." Demon stepped closer. "Not dead. Changed."

She grabbed the door handle as if to warn him of her intentions.

"Beautifully so," he added, hoping to please her. Brutus said his new wife liked it when he said nice things to her. "Your tail is...very...green, like your eyes."

The woman flung open the door and ran.

Demon frowned. He thought it was a fine compliment. She did have a pretty tail. It curved in all the right spots. Not to mention, once she transformed into human shape, those curves became downright delectable.

"Woman, halt!" Demon chased after her, ordering her to stop running. What else could he do? "I command you to listen to me. Ward, I said stop. Come back into my home."

The foolish woman didn't listen.

6

VICTORIA DIDN'T KNOW where she was going, she only knew she had to go. She ran from the large man in fright, over the hard floors of the endless halls. He was a self-admitted demon warrior. That couldn't be good. Not to mention the fact she'd attacked him in the shower like some kind of banshee on crack. Was that a thing? It sounded like a thing. If not, it should be.

Victoria ran faster. Her thinking was beginning to make sense. But she was too busy focusing on mindless matters. Fuck banshees. Fuck crack. Fuck tails, and fins, and demons, and mermaids, and sea monsters, and...

She turned corners, not caring where she was heading, as long as it was away from the demon. She hurried through an archway, glancing around long enough to make sure the room was empty. The stone floor continued across the open area. Mosaic tiles on the wall depicted sea creatures. It reminded her of Moroccan architecture she'd seen at a theme park. The glaze from the artwork shimmered in the light as she rushed past, creating an underwater illusion. She glanced up and realized in fact she was underwater in a bubble.

"Woman, halt!" the demon yelled. The sound of his footsteps quickened.

Victoria glanced over her shoulder as she hurried across the room toward the far end. She ran faster. She didn't feel like her old self. Emotions and sensations filled her, some telling her to turn around, others telling her to run faster.

Suddenly, the floor disappeared from under her feet. Her body flailed as she splashed into a pool of water. She gasped, flinging her arms in an effort to get to the surface. Her body tingled violently, the liquid burning her flesh. She tried kicking, but her legs refused as they had become stuck, fused into one. Saltwater filled her mouth as an unseen force pulled her under.

Drowning. Again.

Victoria held her breath. But it proved futile as

liquid filled her lungs. She grabbed her neck. A fin caught her attention, and she drew her hands before her face to see they had sprouted out of her arms. The tail was back.

Not drowning. Mermaid.

She looked up, seeing Demon standing over the pool peering down. He wore the thin, long towel around his waist like a lava-lava. The water distorted the wavy lines of his image. The burning stopped and the ache subsided. She remained below.

Another form joined Demon, stopping to consider her floating in the pool. They gestured at her, then away, and then back again. The water calmed by small degrees and the image became sharper. Demon's friend had light brown hair and was smaller in size. He wore a toga.

'*Come,*' a voice said. Demon reached his hand into the water and held it out toward her.

Her tail flicked, propelling her back. She did it again, moving farther away. Transforming in the water had hurt, and she was afraid getting back out would have the same effect. Plus, her head felt clearer in the water.

'*They killed Pirene,*' a voice whispered. The voice was not as strong as Demon's had been. '*She was checking on the sea flowers. They plucked one before we could retrieve it.'*

Victoria flung out her arm. It swung her around in the water to see where the voice came from.

'They stole two from our numbers,' another voice answered.

The tone of the second voice scared her, and she darted forward. She grabbed Demon's hand, letting him haul her out of the saltwater pool. The second man handed her a towel. Demon took it from her and stroked her tail, drying it. She grabbed it from him as her legs took shape, holding the towel to her chest to hide her nakedness.

"My lady, welcome to Atlas." The man looked young, and not nearly as scary as the demon next to him. His bright blue eyes shone with kindness. Light brown hair fell long against his back. "Lord Demon, won't you introduce us?"

Demon's black hair had begun to dry. His eyes were inky depths on which light caused a silver sheen. "My lady, may I present you to King Lucius."

A king?

Victoria scrambled to her feet, unsure if she should curtsey or bow. Since she was trying to hold a towel to her naked body, she could only manage a nod. "Your majesty. I am Victoria Jane."

"Victoria Jane," Demon whispered. She gave the man a strange look at the reverent way he repeated her name. "She is my love."

Victoria coughed in surprise at the declaration. Did he say love? Surely there was something lost in translation. Did he mean lover?

The king took a deep breath. "Of course she is. The *Warriors* have been very lucky in finding mates. I should trade my crown to be a hunter, and in a thousand years perhaps the gods will bless me as well. It would seem that is the only way we will be given women." Turning his full attention to Demon, he said, "Please, take Lady Victoria from here. Lady Bridget comes with the young ones. She will not be pleased if there is an unclothed woman in their pool. You know how these women from the surface are about nudity. You are welcome to return once your woman is dressed to present her as your wife. You, of course, have my blessing."

"Mates? Wife?" Victoria repeated, shaking her head. The sex had been good, but come on. That was more than a little fast. "No, I—"

The sound of childish laughter and the pattering thumps of running feet cut her off.

"Many thanks, my king." Demon hooked her arm with his and led her away from the pool.

"You want to marry me after one time?" Victoria demanded as he led her back the way she'd run. Out of all the torturous, horrible, dangerous things she had thought would happen to her, marriage was not on the list. "What kind of hell is this? And what kind of demon are you?"

"We are cursed, but this is no hell." He grinned at her. "Especially now. I told you, you're in Atlantes, and I am a hunter. It is an honorable position. I have been waiting for the gods to bless me with a woman who would want me and so they have. As a mermaid, you understand how it is for us."

She glanced behind her as he led her through the arch. Three young boys ran toward the pool, leaping into the air without bothering to remove their togas. A woman wearing an organza dress that shimmered in the light hurried after them. Her black hair was pinned up at the nape of her neck to create a thick bun.

"I am going to be a hunter, just like our father," one of the boys yelled before hitting the water.

"No, you're not. You're afraid of Mr. Tentacles the sea monster," another answered.

The third boy merely screamed in delight.

It was then she realized Demon had stopped walking. She glanced up at him, seeing his attention on the boys. He stood around the corner, almost hidden from their view. The look on his face was hardly demonic, or scary. In fact, he appeared almost wistful. The softness of the expression took her by surprise.

"What is it?" she asked.

"I enjoy the sound," he said.

She glanced at the pool, hearing loud slaps against the water's surface. "Splashing?"

"Children," he corrected. "It has been so long since our people have had children. In fact, these are the only three in all of Atlantes. Lady Bridget and her husband are truly blessed."

"I don't understand. They look to be about ten or eleven. Did they go somewhere?" She glanced up at the ceiling. Inside, it was hard to imagine there was a dome and endless ocean on top of them.

"No. There is no going anywhere. Once you are in Atlantes, this becomes your home, and none can return to the surface world." Demon sighed dreamily as he finally began to walk again. "We do not know why we have not been blessed with more children. None of the other wives has become pregnant, and I admit there is little to make me believe that we will be so blessed, but yet I hope."

Victoria wasn't sure how to answer. Marriage?

Kids? Mating? Love? "You do know that sex does not equal love, right? And that you don't have to get married just because we did it."

He actually appeared confused by her distinction. "But when you know, you know."

She tried to comprehend the strange turn her life had taken. Now that her head was clearer, she felt she could rationalize what was happening. Several things she knew to be facts—something had punctured the bottom of her rented boat and she'd drowned; she was rescued and carried a long way through the water by a woman with red hair and angry eyes; then they drowned her a second time and she grew a tail. This was Atlantes, the lost city of myth, and many of the Ancient Romanesque things gave the impression she was stuck back in time—the décor, the clothes, mosaic paintings on the walls.

"Lord Demon?" the woman with black hair called. She rushed after them.

Her stark American accent captured Victoria's notice immediately. It was only then she contemplated the sounds she'd heard, though the fact they all spoke the same language was the least magical thing about this place.

Blue-gray eyes studied Victoria as the woman smiled. "So, it is true. We have been blessed, yet again. I didn't know you were at the surface hunting. Did you have contact with the surface air? Did the seaweed work? I thought you were guarding the dome to prevent the Olympians from attacking."

"I was," Demon said. "I did not find her at the surface. The Olympians chained her in the water."

"Chained? So she's not new to Atlantes?" the woman frowned. She blinked suddenly and held out her hand. "Sorry, sorry, my manners. I'm Lady Bridget, or Bridget. I'm not sure I'll ever get used to the lady part." She gave a small laugh. "And you are Victoria Jane."

"Victoria is fine," Victoria answered. "People often mistake my last name for part of my first. In middle school, I hated my name because it made me sound like a country music singer."

"I enjoy the minstrels who play in the countryside," Demon inserted.

Bridget gave him an indulgent smile as she kept talking to Victoria. "So you're from the surface. How long have you been down? Did the Olympians find you and save you, or are they the reason you were lured into the water to begin with?"

"Save me?" Victoria secured the towel more fully around her body and gave a humorless laugh. "Those crazy women gave speeches about loyalty and growing their numbers, and then warned us that they could take our lives as easily as they gave them if we didn't join them."

"Us?" Demon asked.

"It's still fuzzy, but I remember there being more of us in the caves." She studied their serious expressions as they watched her. "Why, who are these Olympians? What did they want with me?"

"Queen Maia must be trying to grow the number of her followers," Bridget reasoned to Demon, before explaining. "Maia leads a group of rogue mermaids who call themselves Olympians. We thought we finally had them contained to the region of Mt. Olympus after they attempted to cave in the dome with earthquakes. Maia has not been pleased. Unfortunately, it looks like they keep finding their way out of the dome into the ocean. We knew they were luring men down to be their slaves, keeping them from transforming into Merr, but this is the first I have heard of their taking women."

"Who knows what sick game they play," Demon said. He touched Victoria's shoulder. "They left her to turn into a scylla."

"I don't think that is what they wanted," Victoria put forth, trying to dig the memory out of her mind. "I think it was a test, or an initiation. At first, I thought they wanted me to fight my way back to the dome, but then I remember hearing someone call for me. Take that for what it's worth though. I also thought I was talking to a girl from my childhood named Becky while trying to redo my taxes. I was whacked out of my mind at the time from being alone in the water."

"So that is what Pirene was doing in the ocean," Demon concluded. "She was sent to gather you from the water and bring you back. She would have succeeded, too, if not for our catching her in open water."

"Yes, Pirene. I know that name. She was gathering sea flowers, or something," Victoria said. "I think maybe *I'm* a sea flower?"

"My husband goes out on patrol today," Bridget said, backing away. "I must go into the abyss and warn him. There may be others in the water."

"Do you need me to see to the boys?" Demon offered. Victoria imagined she heard hope in his voice, or excitement.

"No, the king has them." Bridget dismissed his offer. "Nothing is happening to those three hellions while in Atlas. They can't go anywhere without it being reported back to me."

Victoria watched the woman leave. She was

tired, damp, and needed a nap. Plus, she couldn't remember the last time she'd eaten.

"Lady Victoria Jane," Demon said, grinning at her. "Those mermaids will never hurt you again. I give you my word. I would do anything you require of me."

"Just Victoria is fine." Victoria studied the large man at her side. In light of his expression, it seemed foolish that she had been scared of him earlier. "Do you know what you can do for me?"

"Anything." His eyes dipped down over her towel dress.

"Clothes," she stated simply. "My ass is hanging out."

He leaned over as if to verify this information for himself. "No, I do not think it is, but it is a very fine ass. I enjoy it very much."

"Uh, thanks." Victoria gave a small laugh and tilted her head in a light command. "Come on, Mr. Romance, lead the way."

"My name is Demon," he corrected. "Lord Demon of the *Warriors*. I'm a hunter. Have you forgotten me? Should I take you to the healer?"

"You should take me to a refrigerator," she answered. "I'm starving."

7

"For you!" Demon held his arms wide to present Victoria with everything she'd asked for as he stepped through the door to his home. The kitchen staff brought in fifteen trays filled with every food they had to offer and crowded them on a low table. The king may not be too happy about one of his hunters requisitioning so much of the evening's meal, but Victoria was hungry. Demon had also sent word to the seamstresses to bring all the female garments they had to his room.

He frowned when he realized she wasn't in the room.

"Thanks, brother, I am hungry," Brutus said when the last servant had left.

Demon's expression dropped at the sound of his

twin's voice. Demon grimaced toward the couch as a grinning Brutus sat up to make himself seen. They looked, identical from their long black hair to their matching dark eyes. "Where's Victoria?"

"In the bedroom, getting dressed. Laurel gave her a gown since she didn't have any." Brutus continued to grin devilishly at him.

Demon's frown deepened. He had brought Victoria new clothes and was excited to give her the presents. "What are you doing here?"

"Maybe I've come to make my intentions known to Lady Victoria, your ward," Brutus answered. The man grinned again. "It's only fair. I seem to remember you tried to claim mine."

"She's my woman. Not my ward," Demon answered firmly so there could be no mistake. He eyed the clothing piled on his couch suspiciously. When Lady Laurel had first arrived in Atlas, Demon had offered up his suit by buying the woman clothing. She'd been Brutus' ward, and well, Demon couldn't help himself. Any opportunity to tease his brother had been too hard to pass up.

"Does she know she's your woman?" Brutus gave his brother a mischievous smirk.

"Does your wife know you're making intentions known toward another?" Lady Laurel appeared from

Demon's bedroom. She arched a brow at her husband. Her brown eyes had threads of gold, giving them a unique contrast. Brutus would talk endlessly about his wife's eyes when they were off hunting.

Demon was very happy to see his sister-by-marriage. She made an excellent point. "You can't have two wives."

"I don't think that is in the laws," Brutus said. "If my lovely wife would agree to take another...?"

"It's not illegal?" Laurel hummed thoughtfully. "Oh, well, in that case, she is very pretty."

Demon's mouth opened, and it took a moment to find the words as he was torn between panic and frustration. He could assume they weren't serious. That didn't mean others might not get the same idea. "Victoria is *my* woman. The king gave his blessing. I am going to go announce it right now to make it official."

Laurel laughed. "We're only teasing. Besides, I think the woman has to be with you when you announce. And please, don't just assume she knows what is happening. Human women don't fall in love as quickly as the Merr. We're," she paused to correct herself as she was now a mermaid, "*they're* not built with that same biological knowledge merfolk have."

Demon smiled. Good thing his woman was

already a mermaid. No explanation would be necessary. How could she not feel the bond between them? It was as clear as a beacon of light in dark waters. He had lived long enough to know a good thing when he found one, and the explosion of emotion when he thought of Victoria was unlike anything in his thousands of years. How could that not be love? Why would he question something so honest and simple? Why would she?

"Oh, she doesn't need to go with him. Let my brother announce he's marrying himself," Brutus teased. "He has always been the vain one out of all of us. Like Nárkissos, that hunter from Thespiae. We found him gazing at his reflection, so in love with himself that he falls into the pool each time he sees his own face. Only, he doesn't drown because we're Merr, so he's free to fall in love over and over again."

"I thought Narcissus starved to death because he couldn't leave his reflection in a mirror," Laurel mused.

Demon listened from the hall.

"No, it was a pond," Brutus said.

"Are you certain?" Laurel asked.

"There are very few things that I am certain of. One is my love for you," Brutus answered.

When Demon came back inside, he found

Laurel on Brutus' lap. She kissed her husband softly and gazed into his eyes. There was no way his twin was going to seek another woman outside of his marriage.

"You are my only," Brutus whispered.

"I know, my love," Laurel answered. "Say you're mine."

"Yours," Brutus agreed.

Demon looked away. Seeing the depths of their love was difficult. Victoria hadn't said such a thing to him. Then again, they hadn't been together for very long. He told himself he needed to be patient and wait more than a day. "I am not Nárkissos."

"But you are devilishly handsome." Laurel winked.

"That is because I look like your husband," Demon stated.

"Maybe that's it. I'm going to see if Victoria needs help." Laurel walked back into the bedroom.

Demon craned his neck, trying to catch a glimpse of his woman in the room.

"Why didn't you send word to the country that you had found a woman?" Brutus asked. "Or that you'd been up to the surface hunting without your team?"

"I found her chained on the ocean floor."

"She is *that* mermaid? I heard the rumors when we arrived."

Demon told his brother the details of how he'd discovered Victoria, and how they came to be together. Well, some details he left out, as his twin didn't need to know how they'd cured their affliction.

Brutus stared at him for a very long time, not speaking.

Demon took a deep breath. "We both saw Nemus at the end. If she had been out in the water any longer—"

Brutus held up his finger, stopping Demon from finishing his thought. "Today. You found her today?"

Demon nodded.

"And she said yes to marrying you?" Brutus insisted.

"She did not say no," Demon defended. That was practically the same thing. There was one very annoying fact he'd discovered about the newly married men—they all thought that they had the answers and knew everything about women. "I am sure she feels our connection. She's a mermaid, and will have the—*what did your wife call it*—biological knowledge the same as I do. She is new to being a mermaid, so I would expect it might take her time to speak the words. How long should it take, do you think? Two days, maybe three? I am patient. I can wait that long."

"I wish you luck with that, brother." Brutus smirked.

"Why are you here?" Demon crossed to the couch to inspect the clothes. There were several lacy undergarments, more than any other item. He found himself lifting one to examine it when Brutus' laughter cut off his thoughts pre-fantasy. Demon dropped the lacy clothes on the pile with a scowl.

"Cain reported the death of Pirene to the king. His *Knights* have been called back to search the dome platform for more tunnels. Hrafn's *Soldiers* leave to hunt for scylla. Solon's *Hunters* are patrolling the ocean for mermaids—chained or otherwise. It was going to be our duty, but I was informed we're now going to Mt. Olympus overland to search for Maia and bring her in. I assume the last-minute change in duty is because the chained mermaid is your new bride."

At the sound of Laurel in the doorway, Brutus paused and looked at his wife.

"She's sleeping. That must have been some ordeal she's been through." Laurel went to one of the trays and took a handful of tiny fruit. "I covered her the best I could, but she is completely out of it."

"Out of what?" Demon made a move toward his bedroom. "I will fetch her whatever she needs."

Laurel held up her hand. "Out of energy. You should let her rest. Maybe sleep on the couch tonight."

Demon looked at all the food and clothes he'd brought Victoria and frowned in disappointment. He wanted to present them to her, to show her he knew how to take care of her properly. After a long moment, he nodded. "You are a woman. If you think that is best, I will take your advice."

8

WHEN VICTORIA CLOSED HER EYES, she was back in the office, processing purchase orders and sending work emails in an endless loop that went on forever. When she opened her eyes, she found herself staring at a painted wall depicting a mermaid underwater looking up at the sky.

Dream and reality. Everything was turned around.

'*Will you not avenge Pirene? To do nothing is weak,*' a voice whispered.

Victoria frowned, glancing around the room to see who had spoken. No one was there. She gave a nervous laugh and tried shaking off the dream.

She rubbed her eyes, turning her attention to the opened door. The light was dim. She stretched as she sat up. Her stiff legs made it hard to walk, and she stumbled across the floor toward the living room.

Demon lay on the couch. He was naked except for part of a toga that covered his waist and hips. His arm rested over his eyes. The shadows accentuated the curves of his muscular body. A foot hooked over the back of the low couch. He looked like a marble statue forever in repose, sculpted with perfection. Long hair spilled over the side of the couch, the black trails touching the floor. It was perhaps one of the most beautiful things she'd ever seen.

Victoria stepped slowly around him, watching him sleep.

Glancing around the room, she noticed every artifact had its place, carefully set in its location after much thought—all but the empty pedestal that once held the vase she'd broken. It made her cringe.

Time did not appear to move the same in the ocean as it did above—an hour seemed like days. So long she'd been out in the dark, cold and lonely, thinking of all her sins and, worse, all her missed chances. She should have said yes to more dates. She should have danced more, laughed more, fallen in love more.

But the reality was those opportunities had been infrequent. Men hadn't asked her out on many dates.

Love was a rare thing, and one couldn't simply fall into it because they wanted to. She'd fallen in love with fictional characters, actors on television, men in books. Never in reality. There had to be something there—a chemical, a spark, a blaze that burned so bright it couldn't be stopped. There was no perfect path, for some it was a moment, for others it was a lifetime.

For her, it was now.

Victoria forgot about her fears when she looked at Demon. He didn't move, save the rise and fall of his chest. This moment was locked, a second slowed into what felt like an hour. She could stand and look at him forever.

She walked quietly around the room in a subdued fashion. Her bare feet made no noise on the cool floor. She wore a long, shapeless gown that hugged her curves as she moved. Laurel had been kind enough to answer a few of Victoria's questions. This was not hell. The men here did love. And Demon's mother had given him that name when he was born. Apparently, it had been a quite common name and meant "people as a whole" to the Ancient Greeks. She ran her hand over the empty pedestal. Strange, but not surprising, that this history would turn people into demons.

Desire filled her, not just the physical lust that had caused her to attack him in the shower, but the desire to have a life here. When she looked at Demon, she got him. She heard his thoughts in her head, saw the compassion in his eyes, and understood how lonely his life had been. She couldn't comprehend living a hundred years in the ocean, and he'd been down here for thousands.

She again moved to look at him from a different angle, standing near his head. She lightly touched a strand of black hair.

His arm moved from his eyes and black orbs gazed up at her. A silver sheen caught the light.

"You have the most amazing eyes." Victoria kept her voice soft so as not to disturb the peacefulness that cocooned them.

"They were not always this color. They changed when we were sent below the waves. I don't know why." He gazed up at her, not moving.

She stroked his hair again. "Do you remember coming down?"

"Vague impressions. The past visits me sometimes in dreams. Others are remembered facts that have replaced memories—knowing we drowned, knowing it was painful, knowing that people screamed as the earth trembled beneath us." He didn't move as she touched his cheek.

"You were cursed?"

"We were arrogant," he admitted. His gaze dipped down over her gown, only to lift again to meet hers.

Her hand fell away, and he sat up. The cloth slipped off his hip but continued to cover his lap. She looked at his thigh, resisting the urge to touch him. The material shifted, and she watched as he became aroused.

"Poseidon came up from the ocean and cast us down. Before that, the gods had blessed us with prosperity and a vast empire. Poseidon lifted Ataran out of the sea and made it the center of the world. We were their children and they loved us greatly. Like children, we grew and began to rebel against our parents. We overtook our neighbors, conquered tribes, consumed more than we needed. We thought we were immortal, untouchable. When we had no battles, we raided. When there were no raids, we found other ways to ease the boredom. We thrived more than any empire needed to thrive. Then, in a fit of revelry, King Lucius announced that we were the new gods of our own kingdom and that our land was more beautiful and more plentiful than that of the gods."

"And the gods did not like that," Victoria concluded. It was hard to believe the King Lucius she'd met was that same man. He hardly appeared the arrogant warmonger Demon spoke of. "They cast you down and you became Merr."

"We were cursed for our vanity, condemned to walk only in this sunken paradise, never to set foot on mortal soil again. It was poetic that we were trapped here since we thought our land better than the land of the gods. So here we drift, on the bottom of the abyss."

'*She accuses me of weakness,*' a voice whispered in the back of her mind.

Victoria glanced around, wondering where the sound was coming from. "And you started hearing voices in your head?"

"Aye. I think in a way that must have been an act of kindness, letting us speak by telepathy while underwater."

"Do you hear other people's thoughts when you are out of the water?"

"Aye, sometimes." He nodded. His lips didn't move, but she heard him clearly when he said, '*We've learned to keep our thoughts to ourselves.*'

She studied his face, wondering how he did it.

'*Concentrate your thoughts toward me,*' Demon instructed. '*It's a feeling. You'll know when it happens.*'

'*A feeling. Can you hear me?*' she asked.

Demon nodded. "Aye, my lady, I hear you."

'*This is so strange,*' she admitted. Perhaps the female voice in her head was more like crossed lines on an old telephone connection. "Tell me more. I like listening to your voice."

"This is our eternity, trying to redeem ourselves to a god who may not be looking," Demon said, "imagining a world above that many cannot remember and that has all but forgotten we exist."

"This home is beautiful, and if the land is how you describe, then I'm sure there are things in this eternity that..." She sighed, realizing there wasn't much she could say. What did she know about a thousand years? Even beauty, when seen every day, would begin to fade until the most mundane of another landscape would become desired.

"I would like to show you," Demon offered. "I would like to see it through your eyes. I have a home in the country. The hunters are given estates for when we are home from the waters. I share mine with my brother Brutus and his wife." He lowered his eyes. "Forgive me. I mean *we* share it with them. Of course, the home is yours as well to do with as you please."

"If I marry you." Victoria moved closer to him, standing while he sat on the couch.

"Aye. As my wife." He nodded.

She pushed the hair back from his face. Lowering her mouth to his, she kissed him. She kept her eyes open, gazing into his. His hands found her hips. The material of her gown slid upward under his touch, the whisper of material an erotic caress along her legs. She reached between them, pulling the material from his lap to expose the length of his arousal.

The dim light caressed them with its intimate softness until their movements were accentuated like a slow dance to a song only they could hear—the draw of their breaths, the thump of her heart, the sound of their kiss, the swish of material. When he kissed her, she felt it all the way to her toes. Pleasure built and she didn't hesitate to draw her body over his.

His eyes remained open, studying her with a look of awe and amazement. His body fit into hers as if it was made to be there. They made love gently, letting the passion between them steadily burn. When they met their release, it was a sweet, blissful connection, very unlike the eager claiming in the shower. Demon moved onto his back, bringing her with him to rest on the couch.

Victoria laid her head on his chest. She wasn't tired after her long rest but was content to stay in his arms as he closed his eyes.

After what she had been through at the hands of the Olympians, she didn't want to take a single opportunity or moment for granted. Facing death had a way of making other risks seem less frightening. Demon was a risk she was willing to take, for who knew what tomorrow would bring them?

She wanted to be in this moment forever. "Yes, Demon, I will marry you."

9

MARRIED.

Victoria glanced at her husband. He hadn't stopped grinning at her since the moment he'd brought her to breakfast in the palace dining hall, told everyone his intentions, and then proclaimed they were married. It wasn't exactly the white dress and twelve-tier cake that many girls dreamed of, but then, not many girls married a shapeshifting merman in the city of Atlantes. His smile was infectious, and she found herself blushing and giggling like a giddy teenager on her first date.

A group of them walked beyond the palace, into the countryside toward Demon's second home. Brutus and Laurel came with them, as did Demon's younger brother, Rigel. They all appeared eager to draw her attention to the details of their surroundings as if her wonder could somehow make their home less ordinary.

For some reason, Victoria had not expected to walk out of the palace on foot. She didn't expect to swim either. For a people who'd lived so long, she thought surely they'd have some kind of vehicle to show for it. But, they had no horses, no mechanical engines, only carts that they pulled by hand.

The palace sat on a large hill and opened to the valley city of Atlas. The path from the door to the city was a dirt trail, cut by the endless passing of sandaled feet. The city itself was laid out on a grid system as if someone had measured the distance between streets and placed houses and shops next to each other like building blocks. The only curve was the circular road in the middle of town.

Although such orderly lines appeared militant in their precise design, the structures bespoke of artistic mastery. The walls around the city were blue glazed stones with yellow lines running horizontally through them. Images of sea creatures were carved into pieces of stone, etched on doorways, and tiled into the walls. There were very few people outside, and she was told this was because it was early in the morning.

"So beautiful," Victoria sighed, stopping to touch a carved fish.

"We Merr have nothing if not the time to perfect our trades," Rigel answered. "You should ask Demon to show you his paintings."

"You paint?" Victoria turned her attention to her new husband. What else would she discover about him? "What?"

"The mural in the bedroom," Laurel offered.

"You painted that?" Victoria thought back to the mermaid she'd seen on his wall.

"It is a hobby," Demon dismissed. "To pass the many hours."

"You're very talented," she said. The compliment seemed to bring him much pleasure.

"He is blessed that you think so," Rigel teased.

Rigel was a lighter version of his brothers. His dark hair was not quite black, and his eyes were gray. He was slighter in stature and lighter of step.

The outside was not as she would have imagined. The sky was dark, as she remembered the ocean being, yet it was light within the dome. As they walked, she noticed the brothers fell into a natural formation—Rigel in the front, Brutus falling back to the left, Demon a few paces behind him to the right.

There were no alleys, only stone streets. Since

there were no vehicles, she imagined people had no use for sidewalks. The buildings were tall rectangles with narrow slits for windows.

As they passed through the center, the circular road led them by a statue of a mermaid.

'*We should replace the queen,*' a voice whispered.

"I'm sorry, what was that?" Victoria blinked in surprise and looked around at the group.

"The signs tell you what they sell," Laurel explained as they walked through the center. "That symbol means clothes," she pointed to the next sign, "fish," and then another, "bread."

"Laurel is a very good student," Brutus said with pride.

"I can teach you if you like," the woman offered.

Victoria nodded. A small feeling of distress wormed its way into her at the idea. The writing seemed one step away from hieroglyphics. She'd never been that great at foreign languages.

Demon seemed to sense her nervousness and lifted his arm around her shoulders. '*Don't worry. It will come.*'

They traveled throughout the day until Victoria considered begging them to stop on multiple occasions for the sake of her poor muscles. Rigel often walked ahead on his own as if he was eager to reach their destination. Brutus and Demon spoke to each other in strange half-words, as if they conversed in a twin language no one else could understand, but which often caused great bouts of laughter between the two of them.

"To hunting," one would cry.

"To hunting," the other would answer with a laugh.

Laurel seemed kind and enthusiastic to form a friendship. She clearly meant well, but Victoria had the impression the woman was desperate for a conversation with someone from the surface world. Laurel pointed out various facts she had learned since her swim down. She spoke of oceans currents pushing the dome all over the ocean floor, pointed out birds that nested in the high tree limbs of the forest they trekked through beyond Atlas, and how it was illegal to hurt the rare creatures, for once gone, they would never have birds in the forest again.

Victoria let her talk, trying to cram in all the information as if there was a test later.

As the sky darkened even more and the light shifted from daytime to evening, specks of light danced overhead. Laurel called them sea stars, tiny bioluminescent creatures who were attracted to the heat of the dome. Dark streaks broke apart their dancing as larger sea creatures swam overhead.

"Are we almost to the borderlands you were talking about?" Victoria asked, hoping for a bed and a meal that didn't consist of mystery-meat jerky out of a satchel.

"At this pace?" Demon glanced around thoughtfully. "I'd say about two more days, maybe less."

Victoria stopped walking and looked at him. "I'm sorry, I thought you said you lived in the borderlands. My mistake. How far until we reach your home?"

"I am close to the borders," Rigel said, slinging the pack he carried off his back. "Your home is a little over a day's walk from here." He took out several blankets and tossed two to each brother before keeping one for himself. "See you in the morning."

Victoria looked around the forest. Demon led the way to the nearby trees. She was slow to follow him off the main path. "We're sleeping here?"

"Beautiful, isn't it?" He found a small clearing and laid the blanket on the ground.

"Ah..." Victoria again searched the trees. Rare birds, she could handle. "Is it safe?"

"Yes, the Olympians are not seen in this part of the forest." Demon felt around the blanket, only to lift the edge and pull out a small stick and toss it aside before again patting the bedding down.

"What about snakes? Or bears? Tigers? Lions? Poisonous spiders?" She rubbed her arms. "I went camping one time on," she glanced up, having almost said Earth, but corrected herself, "the surface world and ended up with poison ivy and a snake bite." She was still on Earth after all, no matter how alien it felt at the moment.

"You are not pleased, are you?" Demon gave her a confused look. "I apologize, my wife, I thought you wanted to see the countryside with me."

"I do. I didn't know that meant sleeping in it." She again scanned the trees.

"No harm will come to you. I give you my word. This land is much safer than the ocean, and you survived that."

Victoria looked at the ocean sky peeking through the trees and took a slow step toward him.

"I vow on my eternity, I will give myself to protect you," Demon swore.

The closer she stepped to him, the greater she felt his love for her radiating from him. The fear slipped away, and she reached her hand to him. As she lay down, she found the bed he'd chosen was surprisingly soft. Her aching calf muscles were tense, but she was grateful to be off her feet. Demon pulled her next to him as he looked up at the sky.

"I like your brothers," Victoria said. "You all seem very close."

"We hunt together," he answered.

Detecting sadness, she pushed up on her side to better see his face. "What is it?"

"We had another brother, Nemus. Even on the surface, he'd always been a traveler. When we were banished down below, he couldn't take the isolation. He left to swim the ocean in search of more. That was before we understood who the scylla were. Nemus stayed out too long and lost his way. The sea eventually drives even the sanest man to break. The water invades the soul, taking away everything but the driving need to end our curse.

"The scylla are drawn to life on the surface and wreck into ships like giant waves, trying to be a part of what they once were. Recently, we recovered a scylla from the hunt. After we brought him home and he began the transformation back to what he was, we realized we had found our brother. He died in a cell, as they all do. The Merr are not allowed in the cells when the scylla go, but Rigel's wife, Lyra, had snuck inside. She said he whispered one word, *ocean*, before he dissipated. It took her a week of horrible nightmares to find consciousness after Nemus touched her."

"And you think I might be turning into one? I remember the healer called me that."

"You showed signs but you recovered," he said. "We brought you out of the water in time."

"I think it was the pool in the palace. When I fell back into the saltwater, I felt better and my head cleared." She gave a small shrug. "For whatever that is worth. I'm not sure what it means."

"Saltwater re-immersion?" Demon studied her thoughtfully. "I think we have tried everything, but I will tell the scientists what you say. They are still looking for a cure."

"You said the scylla are drawn to life. Maybe it has something to do with the pool...or the kids swimming in it. Who has more life in them than a happy child?" Victoria turned her attention to the trees. "It really is peaceful. I guess I can see the appeal of camping."

"I will suggest they test the water," Demon said. "I always thought Nemus said the word *ocean* because he was an obsessed scylla, but perhaps it was a message. Thank you for your insight."

"I am sorry about your brother." She snuggled in closer to his side. "To have searched for him for so long only to lose him. The loss must have been difficult."

"Thank you."

As easy as it would have been to slide her hands over his body and make love to him on the forest floor, she found she was content to lie next to his warm body and gaze at the swimming stars, watching for streaks of darkness in the sky.

DEMON AWOKE KNOWING something was not as it should be. Victoria was gone. He had slept so deeply that he'd not felt her move.

"Victoria?" he whispered, sitting up to listen to the forest. All was quiet. *'Victoria?'*

Still no answer. She'd been frightened before they lay down to sleep. He should have paid more attention to that fear. Had she sensed danger in the forest?

Demon stood, moving toward the main path. A feeling of panic shot through him. "Brutus? Rigel? Do you see Victoria?"

Within moments his brothers were searching the forest, calling out to his lost wife. Laurel tried to help, but they made her stay on the path where they could keep an eye on her. They would not lose a second woman.

Demon reached out with his feelings, calling to her with his voice and his mind. She did not answer. He searched the bedding for moisture, scared she might have turned into a scylla and died—an unlikely theory but a fear nonetheless. The bedding was dry.

Victoria had vanished as if she'd never been. He'd promised to protect her, and he had failed. Victoria was gone.

"*Vic-tori-a, Vic-tori-a,*" the pretty voice sang, filling her with such peace and happiness. The pain in her legs from walking all day faded away, leaving only numbness. Victoria followed the sound, drawn to the slender mermaid who sang so sweetly to her. Every note was mesmerizing, leaving her in a trance as she repeated the same word. "*Vic-tori-a, Vic-tori-a, Vic-tori-a...*"

"You've been listening in, haven't you, little one?" Lotis' voice was condescending.

Victoria remembered the woman from when they drowned her the second time. It was hard to forget Lotis' unnerving red eyes, and it was easy to see why Victoria had first thought she was in hell. The Olympian wore a skimpy green robe, so translucent it revealed her naked body. It fluttered as she moved. As much as Victoria wanted to concentrate on the woman's words, she found it hard to look away from the beautiful singer for too long.

"*Vic-tori-a, Vic-tori-a...*"

"We can't have you telling our secrets," Lotis continued. "I have worked too hard, and for more years than you can imagine."

"*Vic-tori—*"

"Electra, enough," Lotis snapped. The song abruptly stopped, and the fog began to clear from Victoria's mind. "I need her to hear me."

Victoria glanced at the three mermaids circling in on her—Lotis the redheaded devil, Electra the siren, with her hypnotic voice, and...

She couldn't quite place the third mermaid's name.

"Carmenta," Lotis stated, pointing at the blonde with purple eyes as if she could read every confused thought in Victoria's head.

Victoria concentrated on keeping the mermaid out of her mind. Lotis only laughed.

"What do you want to do with her?" Carmenta asked. "There is no way I'm becoming landlocked by

Maia again because of some newly finned eaves-dropped where she isn't wanted."

"Aw, she can't help it. Can you, Victoria?" Electra asked, her tone very much how someone would talk to a young child. The cloud threatened but luckily the woman stopped talking before the hypnotic trance could take hold.

'*Demon!*' Victoria thought, not liking the way they eyed her. She had no idea where she was. They were in the forest. It was nighttime. She had no idea which direction was which.

"Oh, no, another disappointment," Carmenta muttered, turning her back on Victoria in disgust. "Looking for a man to save her. Pathetic."

Lotis smirked. "I admit, I had hope for you when I sent Pirene to fetch you from the water. You lasted much longer than the others, which proves you're strong enough to be one of us, but this yelling for Demon to rescue you..." She frowned and shook her head. "That is disappointing, sea flower."

Victoria balled her hand into a fist. She didn't need a man to rescue her. Sure, it would have been nice, but she could do this herself if she had to.

Without giving it much thought, for fear her intentions would be discovered, she swung her arm at

Lotis' face. She hit the redhead square on the jaw, snapping her head back and causing her to stumble.

At the surprised expression of the other mermaid, Victoria used the opportunity to run.

"Get the witch," Lotis commanded. "Stop her!"

Victoria ran faster, ignoring her sore legs and the piece of stick lodged in her sandal.

"*Vic-tooori-ahhhh,*" Electra belted out.

Victoria couldn't resist. The word hit her like a wave of magic, causing her to skid to a stop. It held her bound more firmly than chains ever could.

The stomp of footsteps behind her grew near, each angry sound a warning of what was to come. She couldn't run, couldn't duck her head. A hard object struck her in the back of the skull, sending her flying forward in a daze. The song stopped. She crawled on the ground. Carmenta kicked her in the stomach, forcing her on her back. Lotis stood over her, wielding a big stick. Blood trickled from her lip. The red imprint gave Victoria little satisfaction, considering her current position.

"That is no way to treat your new queen," Lotis hissed. "Bind the witch. We'll use her as bait to lure Maia into the water."

"*Vic-tooori-ahhhh...*"

The loud song drew Demon to a sudden stop in his search. The feminine cry was unmistakable in its entrancing powers.

"Electra," Rigel stated, running to join Demon. "What is that siren doing in this part of the forest?"

"I told Victoria that she was safe from Olympians here. I promised her," Demon whispered, feeling the failure.

"And there shouldn't be any," Rigel stated. He placed a hand on his brother's arm. "How could you have known?"

"I didn't hear her wake," he said.

"I will tell Brutus to take Laurel somewhere safe," Rigel stated. "I don't know about you, but I'm tired of these mermaid attacks. I liked it much better when we thought the Olympian cult was dead."

"I cannot fail her," Demon answered, as his brother went to find Brutus. He didn't wait for Rigel to return before he started running into the forest. It was impossible to tell precisely where the echoing sound came from, but he ran in the general direction, relying on instinct to guide him to his wife.

He would not lose her, not now, not ever. The gods had only just revealed her to him.

AND HERE SHE WAS, at the end of her story, right where she'd began—chained beneath the waves in the cold darkness of the ocean. What a cruel journey the afterlife had planned for her. This was hell, or in the very least purgatory. There could be no doubt now.

They'd let her fall in love, in such a short moment, a moment whose perfection meant more to her than any other in her life. Only they had misjudged. She would not break, not now. She could live on that moment for all eternity because she felt Demon inside of her. He was there, and that made him real.

Victoria knew the facts. Her boat had sunk, she'd drowned once, she'd drowned a second time,

Olympians were evil and she was their toy. This was her afterlife—this endless abyss, dark and lonely, chains keeping her as food for the ugly fish with sharp teeth with glowing dots hanging from their heads.

This was not about Becky Gibson in elementary school, not about her unclean childhood room, nor any small random event in which she did not make the right decision. This simply was the afterlife. How she came to be here didn't matter, nor the why.

When she closed her eyes, she saw hope. Demon. His handsome face. His sculpted body in the living room of his home late at night. The moment she knew she could love him forever. And she *would* love him forever—from right here in the ocean, no longer alone or cold because she had those memories. She would not forget. She could never forget. Love.

The ocean current flowed around her limbs as she rested, and Victoria dreamed of dancing sea stars and dark eyes. Maybe he had been a dream. After being trapped so long in the seawater, she couldn't keep track of the hours. Her heart called out to him to find her again, but the mermaids had swum her farther out and weighed her down with two anchors. The dome was gone from view. The faint beckoning light was snuffed out and she'd been left in complete darkness. She did not know which way to swim. She could not find her way back to Demon.

Weeks. Minutes. Hours. Days. It didn't matter here in the undulating water. All that mattered was the memory that she had felt the love of a demon and loved him in return. Sand touched her tail as the chains weighed her down. Her hands pressed into the rough ground, imprinting it with her fingers like stamps to paper. There was no sleep to be had in eternity.

Oh, but the ocean was vast and endless, lapping away at her consciousness. Blackness surrounded her as her vision faded. So cold. She had the urge to swim, to keep swimming and dreaming. If only she could dissolve from the chains into the water, become part of the waves. She could not fight the current as it pushed her back and forth. And maybe, one day, if she drifted long enough, she'd find him again, the man whose face she held in her heart.

If only she could remember what she'd called him. That man. Love.

'*It has been over two weeks*,' Rigel said, breaking formation to face Demon in the water. His silver tail and fins mimicked the color of ship metal. Though he was the youngest, Rigel acted as leader of their hunting team. Mortal age didn't matter when this far into an eternity. He unconsciously touched the vial he carried around his neck. The liquid it carried would disperse into the water and paralyze a scylla so they could catch it and bring it home. It was the only way they could get ahold of the translucent creatures. '*If she were out here...*'

He didn't finish the thought. He didn't have to. Demon knew what happened to Merr in the water. Even experienced hunters like him couldn't last forever in the ocean, and they had been out for weeks searching along the ocean's floor for Victoria. The land-scapes of the bottom, gentle hills and shifting valleys of sand, were so familiar they began to look the same.

He would search them all if he had to. He would search forever. He would let the ocean take his soul if that meant he could save her.

'*Perhaps we check back with the king,*' Brutus offered. His tail was the same silvery-black color as Demon's. '*She might not be out here. They could have her at Mt. Olympus. We should search for where the Olympians are hiding. You said you heard Electra in the forest.*'

'*Where is your wife?*' Demon demanded of one brother. Then the other, '*And yours?*'

'*Lyra is in the country,*' Rigel said.

'*Laurel is at the palace,*' Brutus answered.

'*How do you know?*' Demon insisted. '*You can't see them.*'

'*That is where I left her,*' Rigel said.

'*Because I feel it,*' Brutus answered.

'*I feel Victoria beneath these waves,*' Demon said. '*She is out here. I must find her.*'

'*Demon, I know you cared for her, but you were not together a long time. Maybe the connection did not have time to form fully.*' Rigel again fingered his vial and glanced at Brutus. The liquid was meant for scylla, but it would paralyze a Merr as well.

'*If one drop of that touches me,*' Demon threatened, '*I promise I will follow in Nemus' path and leave Atlantes forever. You can spend the next thousand years hunting me, only to watch me die.*'

Rigel released the vial. Anger filled him at the threat. They were all haunted by the image of what Nemus had become, and the pain of losing a brother cut them all deeply. '*For you to even suggest repeating the mistakes of Nemus' past is unthinkable.*'

'*For you to take me from my search is even more so,*' Demon countered. '*If I do not find her, I am as good as dead.*'

'*If we do not get back home soon, we will all be as good as dead,*' Brutus answered. '*Saying such does not bring me pleasure, but it is the truth.*'

'*She's close,*' Demon stated. He wasn't sure if it was true, or he just needed it to be true.

What he didn't tell his brothers was that he planned on staying out in the water until he found her, or until he transformed. For, if he didn't find her, it would be because she was already a lost soul. His soul could spend an eternity looking for hers.

Demon swam with renewed force. *'Victoria! Victoria!'*

A small prickling sensation filled him. It was not the first time. It was the same sensation that had made him turn from his pursuit of the Olympians in the forest and move to the ocean. He had lived too long not to trust his instincts, and every piece of him said Victoria was in the water and she needed him.

The desperation became overwhelming. He swam harder, gliding above the ocean floor so fast the landscape blurred. He heard his brothers racing to catch up.

'It's you. Love.'

Suddenly, he stopped as he heard her voice. He twisted around to find her.

Her translucent figure drifted above falling chains. The metal stirred the sand into small clouds in the water.

'No!' Demon cried, seeing that he was mere moments too late. The chains must have slipped from her as she transformed. Only a faint impression of her body remained, a mirage of shadows and light.

Victoria's translucent figure surged toward Demon, as if to throw him back and escape. He tried to capture her in his arms, but the cold rush of her body gushed over him. The water spirit thrashed about to evade his grasp and they gave chase.

Demon had hunted many before her, but there was a desperation inside him, knowing it was his wife. He'd lost his brother to the ocean, and he could not lose Victoria the same way. This wasn't fair. Why were the gods still punishing them?

'*Rigel,*' Brutus ordered. Demon watched his brothers swim automatically into a formation to trap her.

'*Victoria, please,*' Demon begged, knowing as a scylla she couldn't hear him. He thought of his brother, dying in the cell. '*Rigel, we can't. We'll kill her. Brutus...*'

His protests were not heard.

For a scylla, Victoria was young enough and easy to catch. Demon reached out to hold her. Rigel blew the liquid into the water to stop her from swimming. Demon felt his arm paralyze next to her as she stopped fighting. The limb floated uselessly as he moved, but he swept her into his other arm and carried her as fast as he could toward home. The familiar iciness of the scylla's body brought him no comfort. He had her, his Victoria, but he was too late.

He thought about releasing her into the water. At least there she would be alive, but the idea of searching for her for a thousand years, only to end up back at this moment, was too much. She would not want to cause shipwrecks on the surface, hurting people, killing them. There was a goodness in Victoria he could feel. It was in the way she looked at him, in the way she spoke and moved.

'*Demon, let us help,*' Brutus said, trying to take Victoria from him.

Demon did not release her, but he let his brother help him carry her to Atlantes.

The swim felt as if it took too long. She'd made it out of the water once before and survived, but there had still been some sign of life in her body. His brothers remained silent as they moved. There was nothing they could say to comfort Demon. The dome light called to them like a beacon. Rigel surged ahead and was out of the water when the twins brought Victoria into the surfacing area.

Demon did not want to let go, but he allowed Rigel to lift Victoria from the water. All her features were gone and she was just a blur of her former self. The transformation had happened. There was no turning back now.

"I'll take her to a cell and let Gregor know what happened," Rigel said as Demon brushed saltwater from his legs. "I'll make sure he understands to let you into the cell with her as soon as possible."

They had no way of predicting how long the scylla would last after coming from the water. The scientists would do all they could in the holding cell. Sometimes they lasted days, sometimes hours, and sometimes the creature would become lucid, other times they simply screamed in unbearable agony... but in the end, it was always the same result. The scylla died in a mighty splash of ocean water and evaporated like they had never been.

"No," Demon said. "Let me have her. I'll carry her."

Rigel hesitated but didn't fight Demon as he lifted his wife in his arms. His arm began to regain some strength as blood filled his muscles, but he was still weak. He carried her out of the cave into the palace. Gaius the guard was at his post when he emerged.

"Lord Demon, did you find Lady...?" Gaius' eyes moved to the scylla. "You bagged a creature? Well hunted, my lord!"

Demon growled at the man and knocked him out of the way as he hurried through the palace.

"By all the gods, that's not Lady Victoria, is it?" Gaius' voice faded as Demon ran faster.

Demon did not take his wife to the cells. He couldn't lock her up to watch her die. He couldn't let his brothers lock her away, or let the scientist prod at her with no hope of a cure. He loved her. She was his heart. People might say they had only known each other a short time, but that didn't matter. She was his blessing from the gods, and he couldn't give up on her.

"Demon, where are you going?" Rigel demanded. "Come back. The cells—"

"Demon!" Brutus yelled. The sounds of footsteps gained on him. "You do not know your mind."

Brutus slammed into Demon, forcing him into a wall to stop him from running. Victoria's translucent body jolted in his arms. He struggled to keep going, but his arm was still weak from being paralyzed.

"Please, Brutus," Demon pleaded. "I have to try. Nemus gave us the key with his last breath. *Ocean.* We have to try!"

"But the ocean is behind us," Brutus reasoned, clearly suspecting his twin had lost his mind to grief.

"I have to try," Demon repeated.

"Demon, you have to let her go," Rigel stated, slowing his run to a fast walk as he neared his brother. "I know it's difficult, but she is no longer the woman you married. Don't do this to yourself. Let the scientists help her."

"Please," Demon begged his twin. They understood each other in a way no one else could. They had their own language, their own connection.

Finally, Brutus nodded and let go.

"Brutus, don't." Rigel quickened his pace.

Brutus grabbed a surprised Rigel to stop him from following.

Demon carried Victoria toward the saltwater pool. The sound of childish laughter filled the hall. He slowed his steps, breathing heavily from exhaustion. Maybe his brothers were right. Maybe he should take her to the scientists.

"Did you see that?" a young William demanded.

"As agile as your father," Lady Bridget called down to her son in approval.

"Do it again," King Lucius instructed. "You must practice if you someday hope to be a hunter."

William leaped from the water, his blue tail swishing in the air before he dropped down. In fact, his feat was nothing like Lord Caderyn, as hunters never broke the surface in such a way.

"It is time we tested the true value of your seaweed concoction, Lady Bridget," King Lucius said as if continuing a conversation that they'd been having before the boys interrupted. "It is time. With the Olympians attacking, it has become clear that this dome grows too small for all of us. We need options, especially if they try to cave in the dome again. Brutus survived touching the surface air. Now it is time to see if it will allow us to breathe surface air. One of the Merr will be allowed to go to the top."

The green tail of one of the triplet boys flicked out of the water as Gregory remained beneath the surface. Soon, the half blue, half green tail of Douglas did the same, as if the boys competed to see who could lift their tale the highest above water.

Demon stumbled forward, still unsure as to his actions.

"Should I search for volunteers?" Bridget asked, her tone serious as she gave a worried look over her sons. She didn't notice Demon and his burden approaching.

"No. I have the perfect man in mind." King Lucius caught sight of Demon. His words became rushed as he pushed past Bridget. "I will let you know when it is decided."

"Get the boys out of the pool," Demon ordered, his voice hoarse.

"Demon?" Bridget blinked in confusion. "What are you doing? Get that scylla out of here."

"Awesome," William declared, using the word they'd learned from their mother. "That's so cool!"

"A scylla!" Douglas said.

"Can we touch it?" Gregory asked.

"Get out of the pool," Bridget demanded, her expression filled with fear. "Now."

"But—" The boys protested.

"Now!" she yelled.

The boys instantly obeyed as they swam for the edge and leaped out. Demon ran forward, pushing past the king to toss his wife's body into the water.

"Cool," Gregory whispered.

"Can we keep it?" William asked.

Douglas merely stared with his mouth open to see what would happen next.

"Demon? What is the meaning of this?" the king demanded.

Demon watched the unmoving body of his wife in the water, ignoring the insistent pull of the king on his arm.

"How dare you put the lives of the children in danger," the king continued.

Demon stepped closer to the edge, peering in. He could barely make out her shape in the water. *'Please, my love, please.'*

"Demon?" Bridget asked. "Have you lost your mind? What are you doing?"

"It's Victoria," Brutus explained, coming to the edge of the pool.

The king instantly released Demon and moved to look into the water. "Are you sure?"

"We caught her as she turned," Rigel said. "We are certain."

"Oh, Demon, I am so sorry," Bridget said. "Boys, go home. Now."

"But—" Again they began to protest.

"Go!" she yelled and pointed. "And make no stops."

They left, their reluctance and curiosity making their retreat unusually slow.

"The Olympians chained her in the water," Brutus said. "Again."

"Her death is on their hands," Rigel added.

"She's not dead," Demon whispered, willing it to be true. "She's not dead. This worked last time. She's not dead."

"Last time she wasn't," the king paused, as if trying to be delicate, "completely turned."

"I'll go get another vial. When she comes out of paralysis, she's going to thrash." Rigel rushed from the room.

Demon stared at his wife until he determined a shadow to be her hair and another to be her arm. Her face held no detail, merely a shifting glimmer of perception. Brutus had once described the scylla as living ice. Thin blue veins showed inside the watery shell, leading to the faint impression of organs trapped like jellyfish inside transparent flesh. The saltwater pool radiated the strange odor of brine and mud.

"I am done playing fair with Queen Maia," King Lucius stated. "It is time we ended this once and for all."

"What do you mean?" Bridget asked.

"War," Lucius stated. "I am declaring war on the Olympians. Those mermaids have pushed the boundaries one too many times. We tried to be good. We did everything we thought the gods would want —we saved mortal lives, we hunted scylla, we did not lift arms to battle when the times arose. But either they don't care or they're no longer listening."

"We should take her to one of the cells." Brutus lightly touched Demon's arm. "Nothing is happening."

Victoria twitched in the water.

"I have the vial." Rigel rejoined them. "Gregor and his team are on their way."

"Wait," the king ordered.

Demon dived into the water to be with her. The tingling of the shift was automatic as he glided next to her body and ran his hand over her chilly face.

'*Wake up, my love,*' he urged her. '*This water was your idea.*'

"Demon, get out of there," Rigel called, the spoken words distorted by the water. "It's not safe."

What would she do? Kill him? Without her, he was already dead.

He heard the muffled voices of conversation but ignored them. He gazed at his wife, able to picture her face as it had been.

Suddenly, the scylla jerked, shooting away from him across the pool. It crashed into the tile wall before darting back toward him. He heard his brothers shouting orders. He heard Bridget calling to watch out.

Demon opened his arms wide and let Victoria slam into him. He closed his eyes in reflex. She propelled him back with the force of her shove, but he held on tight. His back cracked the tile of the pool.

'*Demon?*'

Her voice filtered weakly in his thoughts—and he opened his eyes to see the pale shade of her face staring back at him. He felt as if his heart would explode in that moment, filled with hope.

'*Victoria.*' He held her tight. Her body convulsed violently, but her temperature began to warm. '*I love you, Victoria. Come back to me.*'

By small degrees, she began to transform. Not into the sick creature of a dying scylla, but into the mermaid he cherished.

'*Demon?*' This time the word was stronger.

'*Demon, what's happening?*' Brutus asked.

Demon couldn't answer. Victoria blinked, glancing around the pool and up toward the surface before settling her gaze on his. She smiled as if she shared his amazement.

'*I'm sorry I didn't protect you,*' Demon said, needing her to know the depths of his shame. '*I should have protected you better in the forest.*'

Victoria's answer was to kiss him. '*How can you apologize? You've saved me from the insanity twice.*'

A splash sounded as Rigel and Brutus jumped into the water.

'*Victoria, are you all right?*' Rigel asked.

'*Let us help get you out of the water,*' Brutus added.

Demon accepted their help as they surfaced. He watched her carefully for any signs of pain as they lifted her onto the ledge. She smiled at him, her eyes tired, but also very happy. He opened his arms to her, still wet and shifted into Merr form as he held her against his chest.

"Where is the scylla?" Gregor, the scientist in charge of the Scylla, appeared.

"There." Bridget dropped a drying linen over Demon and Victoria to hide their nakedness.

"Is this some kind of joke?" Gregor frowned.

"No joke," the king said. "Demon found the cure. I saw it with my own eyes."

"Cure...?" Gregor stumbled to look at the water. He turned to stare at Demon and Victoria, a myriad of questions forming.

Their legs dried enough so that they shifted into their human forms while still holding each other.

"I'll fill you in," Bridget offered. "I witnessed the whole thing."

"We'll need water samples," Gregor said.

"Of course," Bridget agreed, following him as he hurried to get his supplies.

"And don't let anyone else into that water until we've had a chance to—" Gregor began.

"Consider it done," the king interrupted. He knelt beside Victoria. "I am glad you survived. Don't worry. Queen Maia will pay for what she's done to you."

"It wasn't Maia." Victoria glanced at the king. "Lotis, Carmenta, and Electra took me. I'd overheard some of their telepathic conversations about overthrowing the queen and they saw me as a threat. Pirene was one of them. I think she was in the water to rescue me so that I'd join Lotis' gang. Lotis means to be the new queen."

"Dissention in the ranks," Lucius said, standing. "We might be able to use this to our advantage. Thank you, Victoria. This is most helpful. Demon, take your wife home. I'm sure Gregor will come by later to examine her."

"I'll get Althea and send her to you," Brutus said.

Demon helped Victoria stand, but when she would walk, he lifted her into his arms to carry her. She didn't protest as she rested her head against him. He held her close. The drying linen hid her nakedness but fell away from his body as he moved.

"I am sorry I lost you," he whispered.

"You didn't lose me," she said. "I was lured away. I saw you sleeping when I walked into the forest. Electra found me and entranced me with my own name. There was nothing you could have done."

"Why were you walking into the forest?" he asked.

"You don't ask a lady such questions," she answered.

"But...?" Comprehending she was talking about relieving herself in the woods, he nodded. "Of course. To stretch your legs."

Victoria held him tight. Her lips brushed along his neck. "I never want to be in the ocean again, but I know if I find myself there, you will come for me."

"I will always come for you, my love," Demon swore. He turned into the hall leading to their apartment.

"I love you, Demon." Her lips moved over his jaw to meet his mouth. "I need your help with one more thing."

"Anything."

"I'm burning up with the affliction." She arched her brow meaningfully. "And I need you to take care of it before all those people show up to see the former scylla."

He fumbled with the door handle, unable to get it open as her lips claimed his. Her body slid against his as her feet dropped to the floor. Her fingers slid over his to open the door for him. Her hand was on his arousal before they made it inside.

EPILOGUE

Victoria watched the children playing in the pool. The scientists were still stumped as to what exactly caused her transformation back to Merr, and she had become a bit of an Atlas celebrity because of it. Some didn't believe her story since everyone knew scylla could not be cured.

Victoria had also become a bit of a lab test subject. The scientists kept wanting samples of her blood and hair and tears and, well, everything. They weighed her, measured her, asked her to get into the pool to transform so they could watch.

Demon had to order them to leave his wife alone. There was no more information to be gained from pulling strands of her hair. It was finally determined that she was as normal as any Merr woman new to Atlantes.

"Any word?" King Lucius sat on the bench next to her.

"Bits and pieces. They try to lock me out, but some of their thoughts slip through." Victoria kept her voice low, not wanting anyone to overhear. At first, she felt strange acting the part of a spy for the king. The idea of being put back into the ocean terrified her. She knew Demon would always come for her, but worried they would not get lucky a third time. However, if it helped the Merr people, she would risk connecting to the Olympians to hear their plans.

"Anything of use?" He seemed eager for answers that she could not give.

"Lotis and Maia argue. Lotis plots behind her back. I don't know how the queen doesn't hear the mutiny within her ranks. Most of what I hear is blustering and grumbling." Victoria sighed, forcing a smile as one of the boys waved at her from the pool. "I'm sorry I can't tell you more, but I'll keep trying."

Lucius nodded. "Knowing that Maia's hold isn't as strong as it once was does help. I would like to find an end to this."

"To this?" Victoria asked, feeling there might be more to the king's statement than he intended.

"The war, of course." He stood and clapped, cutting her off from prying further as he walked to the pool. "Well done, boys."

"I missed you, my wife." Demon appeared by her side and took the seat the king had abandoned. She wasn't sure how, but he always managed to look at her as if she was the most magical present he'd ever received.

"You were gone for twenty minutes." Victoria laughed.

"I love you." He brushed his fingers against the back of her hand.

"I love you, too." She touched his cheek.

"I have the affliction," he whispered.

Victoria laughed harder. "I'm not falling for that line again. I know that we only get the affliction when we go swimming in the ocean."

"Want to go for a swim in the ocean?" He nuzzled her ear.

"You, Lord Demon, can never be accused of giving up too easily." She turned and lightly kissed him, aware of who might be watching. "How about you show me more of your paintings? You promised me you would."

"I want to paint *you*." He drew a finger down her arm.

"Let me guess." She arched a brow. "I'll have to lie naked on your bed to replace the mermaid that's currently on our bedroom wall?"

He grinned and nodded. "Now that is an idea. You get naked. I'll get the paint. Meet you in bed."

He took off running as if the task was the most important of his life.

Victoria stood, waved at those around the pool, and walked to follow him. When she was no longer in view, she began to run through the halls to beat her husband home.

The End

THE SERIES CONTINUES...

The Merman King

Lords of the Abyss Book 6

Lucius, King of the Mermen, and ruler of the city of Atlantes, shoulders the guilt for his people's curse. After being trapped under the sea for two millennia, the time has come for his people to possibly surface and breathe air. He's ready to be the first to test the theory, but things do not go as expected when a captivating beauty seemingly falls into his lap—and his ocean.

Is Olivette a present from the gods, or a warning to stay punished beneath the waves where his people belong?

Excerpt

Olivette Waller smiled even though she was dressed up like a slutty Mrs. Santa Claus, complete with black fishnet stockings, glitter lipstick, and a tinsel hairpiece that gave the impression she'd made out with a Christmas tree. Though, she supposed that was better than the woman dressed like an Easter bunny who'd fallen on hard times, or the leprechaun who wore more green body paint than clothes, or the Thanksgiving turkey lady with a feather duster attached to her butt.

The party planner who'd hired her clearly hadn't thought of how ill-conceived high heels on a yacht in open water while carrying a tray of champagne flutes was. Then again, maybe he just didn't care. Patrick's Party Events wasn't exactly known for tastefulness. He had, after all, planned a party at sea with the theme of Every U.S. Holiday.

Her legs ached. The breeze from the ocean caused her to shiver whenever she made her rounds along the deck. The red material of the costume felt like a wool blend and had become itchy, with the added bonus of feathery white poofs that stuck to her thighs, neck, and arms. Had this been a simple office party, as she was told it would be, the discomfort would have ended with the clothes.

Olivette had the impression only part of the office was invited—the rich, bloated, drunken, handsy part. But, what was a girl to do? The economy tanked and so did her flower shop. People didn't need bouquets when they were struggling to pay mortgages and buy groceries. Her contribution to the farmers' market helped, but it wasn't enough to keep her afloat.

"There's my little ho ho ho."

Olivette flinched. She'd tried to avoid Tanner Tapert for the last two hours. His breath reeked of bourbon and cigars. He claimed to be the aide of some politician he wasn't at liberty to name. She believed it. He had the expensive suit and smarmy appeal of someone in politics.

"What do you say we go jingle some bells?"

Tanner gave a hearty laugh as he continued his barrage of holiday-themed come-on lines. He'd offered to let her unwrap his present, light his Yule log, and an inventive yet highly inappropriate suggestion involving elves, a tree, and a three-way. She knew he was more interested in showing off for his friends than he had any real attraction for her. Olivette could have been anyone.

Still laughing, he managed to add, "I'll give you a ride on my one horse open sleigh."

Olivette arched a brow and swiped his empty glass from the edge of the boat. She couldn't help herself as she gave him a dismissive once over. "One horse? I'm sorry, I like my rides to have a little more horsepower under the hood."

Tanner's expression fell.

Olivette felt a small victory as the man's cronies laughed at his expense. If he complained, Patrick probably wouldn't hire her back. Glancing at her attire, she couldn't say she'd be too bothered by that. There had to be better jobs.

Only three hours left until the boat turned around and took them back to shore. She sidestepped hands that tried to make their way up her skirt as she filled her tray with discarded glasses and emptied ashtrays. The more she did now, the less she'd have to clean up when they docked. She noticed several of the waitresses taking things a little too far with the holiday cheer, dancing seductively for tips and forgetting their duties altogether as they partook of the refreshments they were supposed to be serving. The turkey had plucked a few of her feathers and used them to tickle the guests, and she'd witnessed more than a few green kiss marks on cheeks from the leprechaun.

"Two hours and fifty minutes until I get to go home," Olivette whispered, leaning against the railing to look out at the ocean. The sun was setting and she could almost forget the party behind her. Who would know if she hid for a couple of hours? Maybe staying late to clean up would be better than trying to weave through the crowd.

She found a private spot near a side rail to watch the water. The music became louder, and the laughter rose to new levels to overcome the sudden rise in volume.

Movement on the surface of the ocean caught her attention. At first, she thought it was a hand reaching up from below. Leaning forward, she squinted into the sunset. The image disappeared, and she gave a small laugh. It was probably a dolphin. No one would be swimming this far out to sea, especially not at sunset without some kind of boat nearby. The boat she was on moved in the wrong direction for it to have been anyone from their vessel.

"If it isn't Mrs. Claus, comedian."

Olivette stiffened as the smell of bourbon and cigars wafted against her cheek. She tried to pull away, but Tanner grabbed her arm. She cried out, but her scream was lost in the chaotic noise of the party. Even if they did hear her, she wasn't sure anyone would come to her aid.

To find out more about Michelle's books visit www.MichellePillow.com

ABOUT MICHELLE M. PILLOW

New York Times & *USA TODAY* Bestselling Author

Michelle loves to travel and try new things, whether it's a paranormal investigation of an old Vaudeville Theatre or climbing Mayan temples in Belize. She believes life is an adventure fueled by copious amounts of coffee.

Newly relocated to the American South, Michelle is involved in various film and documentary projects with her talented director husband. She is mom to a fantastic artist. And she's managed by a dog and cat who make sure she's meeting her deadlines.

For the most part she can be found wearing pajama pants and working in her office. There may or may not be dancing. It's all part of the creative process.

Come say hello! Michelle loves talking with readers on social media!

www.MichellePillow.com

facebook.com/AuthorMichellePillow

twitter.com/michellepillow

instagram.com/michellempillow

bookbub.com/authors/michelle-m-pillow

goodreads.com/Michelle_Pillow

amazon.com/author/michellepillow

youtube.com/michellepillow

pinterest.com/michellepillow

COMPLIMENTARY EXCERPTS

Dragon Lords Series

A Perfect Escape...

Nadja Aleksander has everything she could ever want in life, except her freedom. Skipping out on her engagement, to a man her controlling father has chosen for her, Nadja books passage on the first spaceship she can find. Bound for a planet of primitive humanoid males, Nadja plans on finding a simple, hardworking man who will allow her to live out her days in total obscurity.

A Perfect Mistake...

Dragon-shifter Prince Olek is pleased with his refined and blushing bride. When she chooses him to be her life mate, appearing happy in her decision, his heart soars—until the next morning when his new princess wants nothing to do with him. Olek doesn't know what he's done to upset his alluring bride, but he is determined to reignite the hot sparks that burned the night they met.

Perfect Prince Excerpt

"Come, bride."

Again, she couldn't deny him, moving to dip under the green tent flap he held up for her. When she drew near him, she smelled the warm oil on his glistening skin. It mixed with the natural scent of him. She breathed deeply. This was as close as she had ever been to such an inadequately dressed man before.

She faltered in her movements, glancing up into his eyes. Before she knew what was happening, a strong hand was on her face, gently cupping her cheek. The touch was fire to her already flushed features. Her lips parted with a ragged, scared gasp. Olek took it as an invitation and dipped his head forward.

Nadja almost screamed when he tried to kiss her. Her first reaction was to run. Dodging under his arm, she darted inside the tent. Nadja froze mid-step as she looked around. The red earth floor was covered completely in soft furs. It cushioned her feet beneath her slippers. Below the center point of the pyramid was a high platform bed, which required a step to climb onto it. Silk hung down around the sides, stirring delicately in the torchlight like soft white clouds.

She should have run *out* of the tent, not in.

Spinning to do just that, she realized the only exit was still blocked. She was trapped. Olek grinned, though the look seemed baffled.

"I-I," she stuttered, not sure how to explain her rude behavior, or if she even should.

Olek let the flap fall shut behind him as he followed her inside. He resembled a stalking beast after his prey, relishing the anticipation of the hunt.

Nadja turned from him and was again met with the giant bed. She recoiled from it as if it was covered in poison. It occurred to her how intimate this night really could be. Stumbling back, she bumped into an incredibly hard chest.

She jolted in panic, scurrying away from the solid, warm muscles. Her eyes darted around, taking in the three corners of the enclosure. In the first, there was a bath drawn, the steaming water coming out of the basin. A sweet perfumed scent rose with it. Folded towels, bath oils, and rinses were neatly arranged at the side.

The next corner had a table full of chocolates, fruits and cream sauces. A bench with cushioned seats stretched along the side, resembling a couch. An earthen wine jug was set in the center. Feeling the heady consequences of the liquor she had drunk too much of at the feast, she turned away from the food.

The third corner, behind the bed, was harder to see from her position so she ignored it. Feeling rather than hearing Olek coming up behind her, she again panicked. Swirling to face him, she held up her arms and backed away. Her hands shook. This was not how she imagined being alone with a man would feel like. She always assumed it would be like reporting to one of the robot guards, or talking to a dignitary at some function she was forced to attend.

But Olek was half naked and smiling at her like he knew every thought in her head. Did he somehow realize she liked looking at his oiled chest, to the point where she made a conscious effort not to? Could he know that when his hand had briefly held hers, her nerves had tingled, were still tingling? That the idea of his kisses both excited and terrified her?

Merriment poured from his gaze and she blushed to see it. He held back, standing tall as Nadja studied him. Before she realized it, her eyes were traveling a seductive journey of discovery over his taut chest. Already his small nipples were hard buds. His flesh dipped in all the right places only to rise and swell with each of his shallow breaths. There was no fat on his chiseled form and she doubted they employed beauty services to remove fat cells on a planet like this. His body was all natural. She bit her bottom lip, absently chewing at it as she looked him over.

His broad shoulders carried his strong arms with ease. They were arms that could crush her if he so chose. The metal band on his biceps would have fit on top of her head like a crown. Looking closer, she saw that the jewelry was shaped like a dragon winding over flesh.

Nadja looked at his covered face. He did indeed appear bold and strong like a dragon.

"Are you pleased?" he asked confidently when she didn't move. Again, his smile was alluring and light. She could tell by the expression that this was a man who laughed often.

She blinked nervously, trying to erase the image

of tight flesh burning into her memory. He took a step forward, moving as if to touch her.

"No," she commanded, her eyes narrowing. Her words stopped him. Her breathing deepened. "Just stay back a moment."

His head tilted to the side, waiting for her command.

Nadja took another deep breath, trying to control her undisciplined emotions and wild heartbeat.

"I don't think there is a need to do any of..." She swallowed nervously and looked at the bath and then the bed. Shivering, she tried to lift her hands to cross protectively over her chest and grew frustrated by the binding straps. With a frown, she tugged the belt off her arms. "I meant to say, I know the tradition of this night is to prove yourself a worthy mate by a display of your..."

As Olek arched a brow, she saw the shifting beneath his mask. His eyes dipped to focus on the way her breasts bounced with her jerking movements. She freed herself from the arm ties and left them to hang at her waist.

Swallowing over her embarrassment, she crossed her arms over her chest to break his gaze, and uttered, "Your prowess."

The grin widened over his amazingly firm lips.

Those lips weren't fair. No man should look that delectable. Nadja made a small sound of distress before continuing. She knew he wanted her to choose him for her husband. It wasn't fair. He couldn't really speak until she granted him permission. The only way to grant him permission was to accept him as a husband. Hurting his feelings wasn't a great way to start off their possible life together, so she tried to speak carefully.

"I am telling you, there is no need for that. I am not concerned with..." Nadja felt like kicking herself. The words sounded weak and trembling. Normally she could speak with soft confidence, always reasonable and logical and well-phrased. Her voice came out in hot, breathless pants. What was he doing to her? Her body felt like it was on fire, like she needed to take off her clothes and jump into a snow drift. She started to sweat. Absently, she fanned her face, trying to concentrate. Forgetting where she had left off, she repeated, "I am not concerned with your prowess —*ah!*"

Olek boldly whipped his loincloth from his hips and dropped it to the fur-lined floor.

To find out more about Michelle's books visit www.MichellePillow.com